The Emperor's OSTRICH

The Emperor's OSTRICH

JULIE BERRY

ROARING BROOK PRESS
NEW YORK

Library of Congress Cataloging-in-Publication Data

Names: Berry, Julie, 1974– author.
Title: The emperor's ostrich / Julie Berry.
Description: First edition. | New York : Roaring Brook Press, 2017. | Summary: "Young
  dairymaid Begonia has lost her cow, Alfalfa. So she has set off on a search across the
  countryside even though she has nothing but a magical map to guide her. Meanwhile,
  the Emperor has gone missing from the royal palace in a most mysterious manner.
  Was it murder? Was it magic? It will take all of Begonia's wits to save the empire and
  get Alfalfa home safely"— Provided by publisher.
Identifiers: LCCN 2016038250 (print) | LCCN 2017009478 (ebook) | ISBN
  9781596439580 (hardcover) | ISBN 9781596439597 (Ebook)
Subjects: | CYAC: Adventure and adventurers—Fiction. | Magic—Fiction. |
  BISAC: JUVENILE FICTION / Action & Adventure / General. | JUVENILE
  FICTION / Fairy Tales & Folklore / General. | JUVENILE FICTION / Humorous
  Stories.
Classification: LCC PZ7.B461747 Em 2017 (print) | LCC PZ7.B461747 (ebook) |
  DDC [Fic]—dc23
LC record available at https://lccn.loc.gov/2016038250

Our books may be purchased in bulk for promotional, educational, or business use.
Please contact your local bookseller or the Macmillan Corporate and
Premium Sales Department at (800) 221-7945 ext. 5442 or by e-mail at
MacmillanSpecialMarkets@macmillan.com.

First edition 2017
Book design by Elizabeth H. Clark
Map art by Jennifer Thermes
Printed in the United States of America
by LSC Communications, Harrisonburg, Virginia

1   3   5   7   9   10   8   6   4   2

To the inspiring memory and kindness of
Lloyd Alexander,
And to the students at Mindess Elementary
School in Ashland, Massachusetts, for first
leading me, on March 15, 2012, to

Emperor,
Ostrich,
and Ghoul,

and to the thousands of children who've
brainstormed with me in creative-writing
workshops ever since. To answer the question
you frequently ask me, *Yes.* This really is how
I write a story, and this one's for you.

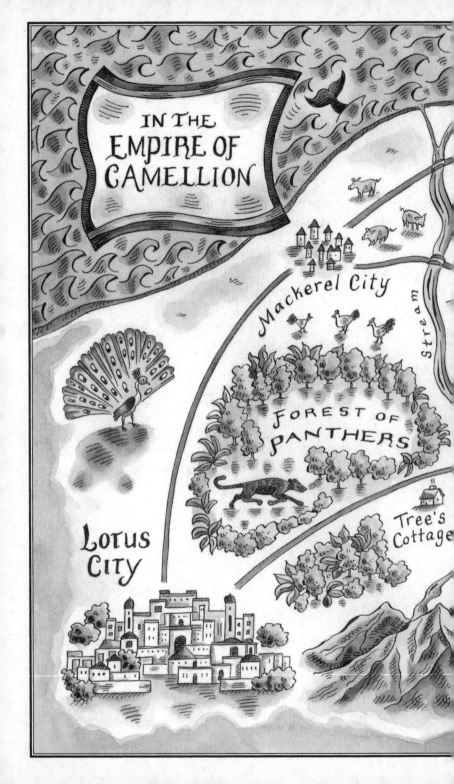

1

OF CATS AND MILK,
AND ROYAL RUDENESS

IDNIGHT, IN THE PALACE.

Quiet lay smooth like a shine on burnished gold, like the nap on brushed velvet. The Singers of Songs for the Evening Shift breathed slowly, then sang again in low, soothing tones into brass pipes that fed their notes into the Imperial Bedchamber. Their voices blended like water in songs so gentle they could break your heart.

The emperor's cupbearer's young second assistant approached the bedroom door bearing a chalice on a tray. Its foamy warm milk surface never stirred. Imperial cupbearers could carry loaded trays across lava fields without the slightest motion rippling the surface of His Exalted Magnificence's drink. Or so they liked to think.

The second assistant bowed to the porter at the door. The porter's gaze moved slightly toward a flank of guards concealed by tall scarlet drapes. The chief guard, dressed in a soldier's gear, stepped forward and motioned to his lieutenant.

"The emperor's milk."

The lieutenant bowed to his captain and removed from his pocket his own less glorious cup. The cupbearer's second assistant poured an ounce of warm milk into the soldier's cup, then wiped the rim of the emperor's chalice.

The lieutenant guard slowly drank his portion. He wiped clean his own small cup and slipped it back into his pocket. They all waited, their ears cocked as though straining to hear the sounds in his belly. *Just once*, the lieutenant thought, *it would be interesting if something actually did happen.* But that something would likely begin with the stopping of his own heart. Such could be the unhappy fate of an Imperial Warm Milk Taster.

The lieutenant rocked back and forth on the balls of his feet. He took a deep, healthy, thoroughly unpoisoned breath.

"Very well then," said the porter to the second assistant. "You will proceed?"

The bearer of the Imperial Warm Milk Cup nodded. It was good of the porter not to treat him like a youth and mention that this was his first time in the sacred bedchamber. "I will proceed."

The porter tapped a teakwood mallet against a hollow silver flute mounted to the wall. A chime hung in the air, then faded. It was answered by a muffled chime from within the bedchamber.

The cupbearer's second assistant felt the muscles in his legs contract. He wiggled his toes inside his shiny new shoes. The porter produced a key from one of his pockets, unlocked the great bedchamber door, and swung it open.

Step after solemn step led the cupbearer's second assistant through the great dim cathedral of a bedchamber, past trickling marble pools where orchids dozed and golden carp flicked their tails, past shocking statues of former empresses and candle-lit shrines to heroic ancestor-emperors from days gone by. Outside, in the palace pleasure gardens, a bird of paradise sang.

A pair of lamps by the Imperial Bed cast a warm red glow upon white silk damask bedclothes. The emperor lay in the middle of the bed, little more than a fitful, restless, thrashing lump beneath blankets and sheets. *So much space around him, and so much luxury*, marveled the cupbearer's second assistant, *and yet he's all alone.*

"I don't feel like milk tonight," said the lump.

The cupbearer bowed and turned to leave.

"Oh, give me some, since you're here." The emperor squirmed into an upright position, and the servant reached forward with the cup to press it against His Radiance's lower lip. Even in the dim light, the cupbearer was dazzled by the luster of the emperor's silk pajamas and the glint of his golden earrings. Rubies clustered like worshippers across his royal fingers, and his face gleamed where the Ladies of Imperial Ablutions had anointed his skin with hazelnut oil. The long tails of his Imperial Mustache curled in divinely royal spirals of blackest jet. These long mustaches were a point of extreme pride for the emperor. Many an older man could not produce such beauties, and he, not yet twenty-two!

Yet for all this magnificent splendor, the young cupbearer couldn't suppress an irreverent thought. *My youngest cousin could wrestle him to the ground easily. And Divine Emperor or no, he still has pimples.*

The emperor sniffed the fragrant warm milk and wrinkled his nose. "Never mind, set it on the table. No. It will spill. Set it on *that* table. No, don't. I don't want it. Pour it out for the cat."

The cupbearer turned, and turned again with each new instruction, keeping his face and the surface of the milk eternally still. In all his training in how to bear, pour, and proffer the emperor's beverages, the cupbearer's second assistant had not fully anticipated how to endure the emperor himself.

"Your Luminous Grace must be looking forward to your birthday," he ventured, and immediately he regretted it, but there was no stopping his tongue now. "Twenty-two is an auspicious age for a ruler . . ." His voice trailed off in terror. *A cupbearer only spoke when spoken to!*

Time quivered like a dewdrop on a petal in the palace pleasure gardens.

The emperor leaned forward. "Who are you," he said, so slowly, so softly, "to address words to me?"

The cupbearer trembled. What would come next? A month

in the dungeons? He held his breath and waited to greet his fate.

"Give the milk to the cat."

The second assistant nearly jiggled the milk in grateful joy. "Yes, Your Radiance. Immediately, Your Radiance. Thank you, Your Merciful Radiance."

"Silence!"

The cupbearer's second assistant turned toward the ivory bowl the emperor had indicated and wondered in his innermost heart if it was too late for him to return home to his uncle's pig farm and live out his days serving more pleasant creatures. At least the emperor didn't smell like a pig. The young servant knelt before the Imperial Cat's bowl to pour. The cat, a gray Persian, lay on a velvet ottoman and watched the proceedings with bored yellow eyes.

The cupbearer tilted the chalice.

"*No!*"

The cupbearer caught in midair the drop that had escaped.

The emperor's chest heaved. He clapped his hand against his forehead, clinking the rings on his fingers. "Why have I never seen? Why have the priests not remembered? *Demons consort with cats!*" He seized the mallet hanging next to the silver flute on his wall, the twin of that which the porter rang, and attacked the flute. Mad notes jangled in the air. He fumed at the second assistant. "Why did you come in here to disturb me with wretched milk?"

The cupbearer set down his tray and prostrated himself

on the carpet. To grovel or to run away and not stop running were his only options. Servants had died for less than bringing milk to a fickle-minded monarch who had demanded milk. Or wishing him a happy birthday. Anger the emperor, and old age might never touch your brow. Or so the older palace servants often said. At the time, the cupbearer thought they were teasing him.

Doors from every direction opened, and servants, butlers, guards, the chancellor, a priest, a dancer, a masseuse, a cook, and a confectioner appeared with the speed of leopards and the poise of acrobats, all armed with the tools of their trades. The cat leaped off its ottoman and dove under the Imperial Bed in one smooth swoop.

"The cat," the emperor hissed. "Banish the cat. Cats consort with demons. Why did none of you think of this before now?"

Jellied fruits quivered on the confectioner's tray. The dancer's finger tambourines jingled uncertainly. The priest took a silent step back and hid behind the cook. Only the cupbearer's second assistant, lying still upon the carpet, could see the cat crouched under the massive bed, its golden eyes reflecting light borrowed from a distant candle.

The old chancellor spoke. "Glorious Lord," he said in a voice that almost hinted that he found these words amusing, "cats have been part of your royal family's lives for generations. Your exalted mother had three of them and found them bringers of good luck. I recall how you yourself had a be-loved kitten when you were young—"

"Never mind when I was young!" shrieked the emperor. "I am *no longer young.* I'm an Emperor in Fullness now." Eyebrows rose among the servants, though this was reckless of their owners. "*Ahem.* Or I will be one in a week. So don't tell me what to do, Chancellor. You know how it vexes me. Now rid me of this pestilent cat!"

The cupbearer's second assistant wormed his body under the bed. In the black gloom underneath the mattress, the cat's reflective yellow eyes stared at him. "*Here, pooss, pooss,*" the cupbearer whispered. The cat made no movement. He stretched out a hand and seized the Imperial Cat by the loose skin behind its head. It yowled and curled its body around to lash at him with clawed hind feet. But he did not let go. He pulled the cat out and held it dangling high. His pig-farming cousins had taught him this trick with their own rat-catching cats. Unpleasant though it looked, it didn't hurt the cat.

The emperor broke off scolding the chancellor and turned to regard the cupbearer's second assistant and his furious trophy. A beautiful smile curved underneath the spirals of his flawless Imperial Mustaches.

"Thank you, servant," he said. A thrill of holy joy ran down the cupbearer's spine. "Henceforth, I pronounce you Imperial Butler. Now I can rest. Banish the cat, banish *all* cats, and bring me new warm milk. *That* milk is now cold."

The original butler melted into the shadows, as did the others who had leaped to the summons. The old chancellor tottered off to the stacks of paperwork involved in actually running an empire. The newly knighted Imperial Butler handed the cat to the Imperial Cat Keeper, an old lady who fled the room before the emperor could decide to execute the Imperial Cat, or all the cats in the empire.

Serenity returned to the bedchamber.

The former cupbearer's second assistant returned with a new chalice of warm milk, again poison-tested by a bored guard.

The emperor drank his milk and closed his eyes.

A cart of supremely irritated palace cats rumbled off into the night. Villagers along their route dreamed of yowling fiends and wondered what curse their nightmares might foretell.

The guards shifted their feet silently and watched their breaths push the red drapes ever so slightly forward.

The new Imperial Butler visited the wardrobe to request the elegant uniform and glittering shoes befitting his new rank. He switched bedchambers with the demoted butler and contemplated sending a letter home to his mother with the proud news. Uncle Moon's pig farm, indeed!

Exotic birds in the palace pleasure gardens settled into their nests and tucked their lordly beaks under their riotously colored wings. Peace and order reigned supreme.

And then . . .

Somewhere in the smallest hours, a tortured scream ripped through the quiet palace. To their astonishment and horror, no one, neither guard nor dancer nor baker nor butler, could open the doors to the Imperial Bedchamber to help. The peepholes that allowed the guards to monitor the emperor's safety had been fused shut. Any hand that dared to touch the latch of the emperor's door burned with a red-hot brand, leaving a wound slow to heal.

Guards pounded and cursed. Servants paced and prayed. Dark forces must be at work.

How dark, indeed, they couldn't fully know until the next morning, when the locks finally yielded and the new butler found the Imperial Bed empty and its sheets disheveled. The emperor himself was nowhere to be seen. His gold ear jewels and ruby rings lay on the floor near his bed.

One window stood open, and the butler ran to see what it might reveal. Outside in the palace pleasure gardens, not a flower was out of place, nor a creature disturbed.

Except, they learned later, for one. With hordes of servants scouring every corner of the castle and grounds, scarcely anyone took notice when, at dinnertime, the Keeper of the Imperial Aviary reported one missing ostrich.

2

WHAT A PEACOCK MIGHT HAVE HEARD

IF A PEACOCK HAD BEEN STRUTTING NEAR THE Pools of Celestial Vision in the gardens outside the Heavenly Hall of the Ancestors not long before the emperor disappeared in the small hours of the night—if hours even matter in the Heavenly Hall, and who can say?—he might, if he'd listened, have overheard this conversation.

A grandfather spirit perched precariously upon the head of a dragon statue, frowning into the tranquil waters, with his chin sinking irritably into his hand.

"Did you see that? Did you *see that*?"

The peacock might have turned his beaky face this way and that, as peacocks do, searching to find the person the grandfather spirit was speaking to, until a grandmother spirit in fluttery, pearly robes blinked into view upon the dragon's spine.

"What, dearie? See what?" She squinted into the waters. "Oh. Him? You're the only one who bothers with watching him. I have the loveliest great-great-great-granddaughters right now, and I'm so taken by the clever things they do. Why, just this morning—"

"He banished a cat!"

The grandmother spirit paused. "He did?"

The grandfather spirit nodded. "He's not even sorry. He's sleeping now, without a care in the world."

"Well," the grandmother spirit said briskly, "this can be fixed. If he unbanishes the cat, apologizes enough, and offers enough treats, in time, he'll be forgiven. The bad luck . . ."

"He's got the heart of a rotten onion and the spine of a soup noodle."

"Mmm, noodles . . . I miss noodles."

"Stop changing the subject with food." The grandfather spirit climbed to his feet and stood on the dragon's impressive snout. This would've upset the peacock, no doubt, but by then a peahen would likely have appeared, and the peacock would've fanned his feathers and strutted for her entertainment, forgetting all else. Silly, vain peacock!

"His twenty-second birthday feast is soon," the grandfather spirit said darkly.

The grandmother beamed. "Emperor in Fullness! How nice."

But the grandfather could only growl. "He's *not* ready.

Can you imagine what will happen to the empire when the chancellor turns the scepter over to him?"

The grandmother spirit shrugged. "He'll have to start leading and learning from his mistakes the way all emperors do." She smiled. "I remember a Full Emperor's Scepter Feast when I was young. Let's see, now, what was that emperor's name? The tall one. He was so handsome, we girls all thought. They put paintings of him on banners throughout the empire."

The grandfather spirit waved his finger high in the air. "I've had it with the little toad. He's a disgrace to the family."

"Patience, old friend. You know what comes of getting angry. Havoc, that's what."

"The time for patience is past. The fate of the empire hangs in the balance. It's time someone taught that selfish rat a lesson."

The grandmother tugged at his sandaled feet. "Sit down. A toad, a rat . . . he's a mortal. Don't expect too much. Besides, it's not your concern. Leave life to the living, I always say. Have you done your serenity exercises yet today?"

"You're always fussing at me. There's a time for serenity, and there's a time for action."

The grandmother spirit sighed. She blinked out of sight, reappearing moments later in a meditative pose, floating on a tiny lily pad in the pool.

"What are you planning?" she inquired. "That look of yours always worries me."

Silence.

"You *know* we're not supposed to intervene."

"But we *can* intervene." And with a twiddle of his fingers, the grandfather spirit vanished, leaving the grandmother spirit alone with her troubled thoughts.

"You'd drive me to my grave if I weren't dead already," she muttered to her absent companion. "You know how it irks me when you make me break the rules." She peered thoughtfully into the pool until a small smile spread across her lips. "Now I shall have to intervene, too, and send a helper along. I know just the girl for the job." And she was gone.

This is what a peacock would have heard if he'd been listening to this conversation in the gardens outside the Heavenly Hall of the Ancestors. But since peacocks can't understand a word that's spoken, the ancestor spirits' plans would remain a secret. For the time being.

3

INTERVENING,
AND A PECULIAR PAIR

OMENTS LATER. ONE MINUTE, PERHAPS, but not a feather more than two.

In the aviary, beyond the pleasure gardens, amid peeps and mutters and ruffling feathers, the birds of the Imperial Menagerie slept.

One ostrich, a splendid young male, found his sleep plucked away from him. Something hovered close beside him in the darkness, but not even the ostrich's enormous eyes could spot it. It stroked his back feathers, though, and the ostrich liked that.

"I have a mission for you, Friend," the something said.

The ostrich could no more understand words than bake a cake, but a picture filled his mind of a person, short and scrawny. Like an ostrich chick, if one thought about it with a very small brain. He could see him. Hear his voice. Smell his smell.

"Find him. Keep him safe."

Urgency. The ostrich felt it shooting through his long limbs. This human was his, now. He must find his man-chick. Never mind that this young ostrich had never yet found a mate, much less guarded a chick of his own. A father ostrich's protectiveness now surged through him. He rose and spread his sheltering wings. He was ready to run and, if need be, fight.

The presence in the darkness was gone. The ostrich sensed its absence like a change in the wind. But the memory, the urgent call, remained.

Find him.

He stalked through the aviary, finding the gate to his pen and the door to the outside gardens both flung wide open. This was odd, but asking why was not his specialty. He roamed the grounds, ankle-deep in wet grasses, listening.

Time passed. Not finding what he sought made him ache.

Find him.

Then, something. His plume feathers prickled. What was it? What?

A scream ripped the night.

Danger! A jackal? A panther? A hunter? Some threat to his man-chick? The ostrich began to run. His mighty legs propelled him forward.

There, at the palace itself. Light spilled from a tall window.

It burst open, and a form scrambled out. It tried to sidle away from the window on a narrow ledge but slipped and fell, only just catching itself with its legs dangling in the air.

But not too high. Just high enough for the ostrich to run to his man-chick and hoot at him reassuringly. The human screamed again and let go, landing on the ostrich's back with his legs tucked under the great bird's wings, as if some unseen hand had placed him exactly there.

"Yeaagh!" cried the man-chick. He clutched the long neck for dear life.

But the ostrich didn't mind. He took off at a gallop, unbothered by the puny weight of his passenger. When he reached the palace gates and found that they, too, were open wide, the ostrich took off along the hard-packed gravel of the road. The twinkling lights of Lotus City, capital of the blessed empire of Camellion, beckoned below, but the ostrich skirted another way around the palace hill and took a dark path toward the countryside, with its comforting birdcalls and cricket songs. Astride his back, the human shrieked and moaned and shivered with fright.

The ostrich submitted patiently to the aggravation and pressed on through the night. He had his charge, and that was what mattered. Soon the poor thing would settle and sleep. There was all the time in the world for the youngling to learn that his papa ostrich would protect him.

4

A MILKMAID, AND HER WANDERING COW

A SUNNY MORNING, FIVE DAYS LATER.

"Alfalfa's gone missing again, Begonia."

Oh, that cow!

Their other cow, a crabby old lady named Cud, swished her tail in Begonia's face while Begonia kneaded her udder with strong fingers. Cud splayed her hind legs a bit wider, making her milk-bag harder to reach. Begonia shoved her shoulder into Cud's side and milked with grim determination.

"Did you hear me, Begonia? Mumsy said you'll have to go find Alfalfa and bring her home. Grandmother Flummox is sick again, so Mumsy's making her soup."

The dairymaid sighed and faced her younger sister. "I hear you, Peony. My ears still work."

Pink morning sun peeked through the slats in the barn

wall. The spring air smelled of fresh morning dew and sweet hay and warm cow breath.

Peony stroked Sprout, Alfalfa's new calf, along her soft side. "Mumsy says you'd better find her quickly," she said, "before she eats another of Madame Lili's pear tarts."

"Find her yourself," Begonia called. "And muck out her stall!"

Peony stuck out her tongue in reply and left the cow dung, as always, to dependable Begonia. Peony had probably never gotten cow poo on her boots in her life. Her black curls swished over her shoulders as she left the barn, though why a young dairymaid would wear hair that bounced all down her back was more than Begonia could figure out. Cows might just eat hair like that. Especially a cow like Alfalfa.

Alfalfa was a curious cow. It was true; once she wandered to the village temple and ate the priestess's afternoon snack. It was odd, though, Begonia thought, for Alfalfa to roam now, with her calf so young and needing her milk.

"*I* shoveled and milked when I was nine," Begonia muttered to the empty barn. "I've weeded the garden since I was six."

Hay, Cud's calf, mooed in reply. Hay and Sprout had heard Begonia's song of woe before.

"She *should* go find that foolish cow," Begonia went on over the shooshing of milk in her pail. "Mumsy should make her."

But Peony was too young to wander over hill and dale in search of a vagabond cow, and Begonia knew it. Mumsy—more precisely, Chrysanthemumsy—would never hear of such a thing. The way Mumsy spoiled Peony was maddening, but there was no getting past those curls and dimples.

Begonia made a mental list of what to do next: find a hat, fill a canteen, pack a slice of bread and maybe some cheese. Hunting for Alfalfa could take time. This wasn't the list she'd wanted for today. She had planned to spread manure over the vegetable beds, hoe the soil, and water her indoor seedlings in their pots, after feeding her chickens and gathering eggs. A much more satisfying schedule.

She hefted her bucket of milk and turned toward the door. She'd barely taken a step, though, when something hard struck her bottom with the force of a cannonball. She toppled forward in the straw, landing face-first in a new puddle of creamy milk.

Her pail lay on its side, and Cud chewed her—well, her cud—with the placid contentment of a cow whose kick has met its target.

Begonia climbed to her feet and shook milk from her hair. She swallowed a few choice words for Cud. Why waste breath on an ill-tempered beast? It was her own fault. She'd let herself be distracted. Begonia surely knew better than to pass behind those kicking hooves. Not that she would pardon Cud's meanness anytime soon.

She rubbed her sore bottom, then headed for the house and went inside.

Catnip, the cat, lay snoozing in a windowsill. Mumsy

looked up from kneading bread dough at the empty pail, then at her daughter's face. "Did Cud have one of her moods again?" She chuckled. "Silly old cow."

Begonia scrubbed her milky, dirty face with a wet cloth. "Silly? That *silly* old cow has given my bottom a bruise that may never recover."

Mumsy pushed her own hair out of her face with a floury hand. "Good thing, then, it's hidden where the sun won't shine. Stir the pot, will you, Begonia?"

Begonia stirred with one hand and rubbed her sore bottom with the other. "*And* she knocked over all the milk."

Mumsy waved this away. "There's always another day and another pail. Besides, you got a nice yield from Alfalfa this morning before she left for her little stroll."

Begonia scowled. Easy enough for Mumsy to sound unconcerned, but Begonia knew they needed that milk. If they couldn't sell their cheese and butter at the weekly market in Two Windmills, they would have nothing else to live on. Her garden wouldn't begin producing vegetables for months yet. Except for lettuces, and they couldn't live on lettuces alone. They weren't rabbits.

Peony climbed down the ladder from the sleeping loft with a hairbrush in her hand. "Brush my curls, Mumsy?"

"In a minute, baby," their mother answered.

Baby! Combing curls. *Tchah.* Begonia didn't envy Peony. Not exactly. She wouldn't want to be her flouncy, spoiled sister for a hundred silver buckles. She'd much rather be a strong farm girl than a porcelain doll. But sometimes the festival of adoration between her and Chrysanthemumsy was hard to take.

"I've got to get this dough rising, and I still have lots of chopping to do for the soup. Poor old Grandmother Flummox! Her cold is taking days to mend. But that's what happens when you grow old."

Begonia leaned over the dirty water bucket and wrung more milk from her own uncurly hair, then snatched a dry heel from last week's bread, smeared it with soft butter, and gnawed on it. She knew it was right and proper of her mother to take soup to their elderly neighbor. More than right and proper, it was something Mumsy's generous soul could never overlook. But Begonia wished, in her secret heart, that Mumsy wasn't always so busy. If she weren't, or if Peony could help look after the farm as a girl her age should, Mumsy could come along on the stroll to find Alfalfa, and what a treat that would be.

"Peony could chop your vegetables," Begonia told her mother.

"Oh, I'll just do it," Mumsy replied. Begonia looked away. Once again, Peony was spared any effort.

Chasing Alfalfa might be just the change of scenery Begonia needed today. And maybe, if she was gone long enough, Peony would be forced to dirty her sweet little hands and do some work. Though she doubted it.

"Don't forget Alfalfa, Begonia," Peony called to her. "Mumsy, have you embroidered my new hair ribbons for the emperor's birthday ceremony tomorrow?"

Begonia banged out the door before she could hear the answer.

5

CURIOUS ENCOUNTERS, AND DUBIOUS GIFTS

IT WAS THE KIND OF FRESH, SPARKLY MORNING that might make a young girl forget the milk oozing over her scalp and the ache in her bottom. Mist swirled over the blossoming grasses and clover, and birds twittered and chased one another in the hedgerows. Rising sunlight gleamed on spiderweb dewdrops. It ought to have been a day brimming with hopeful possibilities.

Chasing Alfalfa across the countryside was not on Begonia's list of hopeful possibilities.

She started out in the direction of Alfalfa's usual haunts and called out to a neighbor for help through his open window.

"Master Mapmaker, have you seen our white cow, Alfalfa? She got away again this morning."

The master mapmaker poked his head out the door of his small house. He blinked through his enormous round spectacles, which gave him bulgy-looking eyes. Begonia bowed to greet him.

"Which flower are you, again?"

"Begonia." Nobody could ever remember "Begonia."

The master mapmaker's braided gray beard hung in a pointy rope all the way down to the silver watch chain that stretched across his blue vest and round belly.

"I did see an errant cow earlier this morning, Maid Begonia," the mapmaker said. "She was headed in a west-by-northwesterly direction, along this very road you're traveling. White, you say? With a black mark on her forehead shaped like a compass?"

Begonia nodded, though she wasn't sure about the compass. Mumsy said Alfalfa's marking looked like a flower, but then, of course, she thought everything looked like a flower. Even her daughters. He must mean Alfalfa. What other white cow could it be?

"Then your Alfalfa cow passed by here not long ago, Maid Begonia. Perhaps half an hour. She tends to wander, doesn't she? Are you sure you want to go after her alone?"

Begonia didn't want to, frankly, but there was no point telling Master Mapmaker that, and as sure as flies in a cow's eyes, Mumsy wasn't going to change her mind and join her. "It's no trouble," she told him. She thanked him and turned to go.

"Wait!" the mapmaker cried. He shuffled through piles of

parchments on his desk, then handed a smaller one to her. "Take this with you. In case you need it."

Begonia studied the drawing in her hand. It was a map of the countryside around their village of Two Windmills (though now there was only one), but she herself had never seen a map. Why should she need a map for the very place she'd spent her whole life? She knew every house, field, creek, and tree for miles around. Yet this drawing made it look different somehow. Smaller and more curious, with each dwelling and barn and temple etched in intricate, colorful detail. The map lacked any writing or labels, but its pictures were sharp and vivid. There was the windmill by the waterfall in the creek. There were the remains of the broken one. The map even had animals sketched in, peacocks and cows and panthers and pigs. She would hang it next to her bed, she decided, and enjoy gazing at it. Though only a map, it reminded her of sacred paintings in the temple. She'd never owned her very own bit of art. It made her imagine things, and wish for some paints of her own.

"It's only a sketch," the mapmaker said. "Something I did to pass the time. But you never know when a map can be useful."

"Many thanks, Master Mapmaker," cried Begonia. She slipped the little scroll into her pocket and hurried off, west-by-northwest.

Half an hour of a cow strolling. How far was that? And how long should that take an energetic girl? She quickened her pace and admired the blue of the sky. If she had all the paints and inkpots and paper that Master Mapmaker had, she would try to paint a blue to match that sky, with shades of green for trees and fields.

Green was everywhere. Thank goodness cows weren't green, or she'd never find Alfalfa. There were a thousand places something green could hide in the lush spring countryside. But a white cow shouldn't be hard to spot.

Alfalfa the cow, however, proved very hard to spot.

The sun climbed in the sky, and Begonia climbed the long, steep hill that led toward the village center and the windmill by the creek. Chickens pecked and clucked in front of cottages, and skinny, tousled children toddled out into their front yards to gawk at her as she passed. There was something nice about roving about in the wider world, Begonia thought. A little freedom was so satisfying. Peony, for all her curls and kisses from Mumsy, didn't get to see the world pass by as Begonia got to.

A small barrow rattled by, wafting pungent scents. Peering around its sides was a short, wrinkly old woman wearing a magenta scarf, with wispy white hair escaping the bun at the back of her head.

Begonia bowed to the old woman. "Madame Mustard-maker," she said. "I'm searching for my white cow, Alfalfa. She's lost."

"Flower girl!" the old woman cried. "You taste my batch and tell me, is it good?"

Before Begonia could protest, the bent figure had torn a bit of bread off a long loaf, whittled a slice of cheese off a fat wedge, and spread the whole creation with a brown and speckled mustard paste. Begonia had been raised too well to even think of declining this invitation from a respected village elder. Madame Mustard-maker was a beloved fixture in Two Windmills. Begonia took a bite.

Flames erupted in her mouth. Or so it seemed. Tears flooded her eyes. Manners or no manners, she opened her mouth and panted to cool her tongue.

Madame Mustard-maker watched her anxiously. Her eyes crinkled with worry. "Too spicy, just a tad, do you think?"

Begonia's manners returned, just enough. "Oh, no," she managed to say just before a thread of emergency drool escaped from her lower lip. "Ith deliciouth."

Madame Mustard-maker beamed. "I *knew* today was a good day for mustard-mixing. I felt it in my elbows."

Begonia swallowed hard.

Madame Mustard-maker took a small clay pot from somewhere in her barrow and spooned in her sticky brown mustard mixture until it was full. She stoppered it with a fat cork, then wrapped the whole jar in an old cloth. "For you, flower girl," she said. "Keeps you healthy." She pressed it into Begonia's hand and wrapped her fingers around it protectively. "Your cow. The one with the spoon on her forehead. She marched right through town, not an hour ago."

Begonia didn't dare refuse the gift of mustard. She thanked

the old woman, then knotted the mustard pot into her apron. *Spoon?* she wondered. *An hour ago?* She was losing ground. Alfalfa was winning this slow footrace, apparently.

The mustard-maker turned to leave, then paused and wound her own magenta scarf around Begonia's slightly sticky head.

Begonia was so startled she forgot to offer thanks. The mustard-maker winked at her and rattled off, pushing her cart. Begonia examined the scarf. Though a little worn, it was still the brightest thing in sight. The wind caught it and ruffled it out behind her like a kite's tail as she headed down the road.

She reached the village proper, and hurried up and down its short, winding streets. No sign whatsoever of a wandering cow. She made her way to the grassy space at the center of town, where children played, grown-ups gossiped, and merchants sang about their silver, soups, and sandals. Conversation buzzed today, as Two Windmills prepared itself for the emperor's twenty-second birthday celebration. Tomorrow would be a grand ceremony, and the following day, the birthday itself, there would be a feast.

But amid the bustle, there was still no hint of a cow. Yet Madame Mustard-maker had said she'd seen her. Begonia decided to ask once more.

"Excuse me," she said to the Seller of Many Things, whose little tent sparkled with shiny oddments that twisted and turned in the breeze. "I'm looking for my lost cow, Alfalfa. Did you see her pass this way this morning?"

The Seller of Many Things hung a set of wind chimes from a tent rope and rubbed his round chin. "Do you mean a white cow with a violin-shaped spot on her forehead?"

By now, Begonia wouldn't have been surprised to hear that Alfalfa's spot looked like a portrait of the emperor. She nodded.

The chimes tinkled as the Seller of Many Things answered. "I saw that cow pass through town today. Probably an hour and a half ago. She seemed like a traveler with a long road ahead of her, marching straight along. Not like your usual wandering cow."

Begonia's heart sank. How could she keep on losing ground to a cow? And where might Alfalfa be going?

She tried to think. This might turn out to be a much longer journey than she'd realized. It could take the better part of the day to catch up to Alfalfa and lead her home. She'd need food and water, or some money to buy them, and she had neither. If only she hadn't barged out the door this morning before gathering supplies! But if she returned home now to prepare for a journey, then retraced her steps, Alfalfa would get ever farther away. There was no telling where the cow might end up. At least, thus far, she'd kept to the road. But there was no reason to suppose she'd remain on it.

What to do? Without her calf to nurse, Alfalfa would need

a milking desperately. Her milk-bag would be painfully full before the day's end. And poor Sprout, home all day and growing hungry!

"There now, why the sad face?" inquired the Seller of Many Things. The gold hoops dangling from his earlobes shone like the dome of his shiny bald head.

"My cow keeps getting farther and farther away from me," Begonia told him. "I need to find her soon, or she'll be hopelessly lost." *And so will I.*

The Seller of Many Things nodded. He untied a ribbon on which a small brass bell dangled. "Here," he said. "Take this bell. No, I don't need money for it. When you do find your cow, tie it around her neck, and that way she'll be easier to find the next time."

Finding Alfalfa *next time* was the last thing on her mind. If Begonia had her wish, there'd never be a next time. Mumsy should hire a blacksmith to forge a chain that would tether Alfalfa permanently to their own small pasture. No, they couldn't afford that. But they could sell Alfalfa and use the money to buy a less adventurous cow.

She fingered the brass bell. Her sweaty palm muted its tinkle, so she held it by the ribbon and swung it aloft. A lilting chime floated across the green.

The Seller of Many Things winked. "Hear that? Louder than you'd think. It might be a magic bell."

"Thank you," Begonia said. She tried to smile, but the

empty road tugged her gaze, winding away from the center of town and downhill into the lowlands north of Two Wind-mills.

"Have a drink, before you go," the man said, and he pointed toward a ladle extending from a pail. Begonia saw the wisdom in this and took a long, quenching drink of water. Then she pulled Madame Mustard-maker's scarf over her forehead, tucked the bell into her apron along with the mustard pot, thanked the Seller of Many Things once more, and hurried off down the road.

She pushed her feet faster and faster. *Catch that cow! Catch that cow!* Speed was her best hope. Refreshed by the water, she felt sure she could make up for lost time. But as the morning sun rose in the sky, and the road wandered on and on, and the farm plots and barns began to feel less and less familiar, doubt became Begonia's traveling companion. The pair was soon joined by despair. On an errand such as this, Begonia would have preferred to travel alone.

But it was not to be. Her footsteps brought her through the small Hamlet of Mossy Well. She saw the fabled well and peered into its green depths. It waters had once healed an ailing empress, but Begonia decided against drinking its algae waters now. More miles of walking brought her through the settlement of Radish Row. Farmers hoed their vegetable fields and thinned leafy rows. A matronly woman offered Begonia a crunchy early radish, and she ate it gratefully, but it needed a better washing, and its bite made her tongue burn.

She left the settlement behind and tried to use the magenta scarf to better shield her face from the sun. The road dipped down around a small hill and out of sight. Begonia followed the curve in the road and came, to her surprise, to a wide fork. The road to the left headed toward a distant forest. To the right, the road rolled over miles of pasture. Surely Alfalfa would choose such a sea of succulent grasses. Still, Begonia hesitated.

A woman approached from the grassy road to the right, carrying an infant in her tired arms.

"Greetings, good mother," Begonia called to her. "May I ask you a question about what you've seen on your long walk?"

"You may," said the woman, "if you'll hold the baby." Without waiting for an answer, she thrust her bundle at Begonia.

The child was squirmy and slightly damp in ways Begonia preferred not to think very hard about. She jostled his weight. He gazed up at her through wise, dark eyes and gurgled at the sight of her bright, waving scarf.

The mother, meanwhile, moaned and stretched her arms, shoulders, and back.

"You must've been walking a long time," observed Begonia.

A loud crunching sound escaped from her spine as the mother cracked her neck. "It is what it is. I've walked since sunup, I'll have you know. We're on our way to visit my grandmother. She's an old widow, and I'm a young one."

"I'm sorry." Begonia gazed once more into the baby's eyes. Poor little mite, without any papa!

The woman shrugged. "It is what it is."

The baby jabbered, and Begonia smiled. The mother, meanwhile, dropped down onto the ground and stretched out her legs. Then she rolled onto her side and closed her eyes.

Begonia realized she might end up tending this infant all morning if the tired woman went to sleep. "Good mother," she cried loudly, "here is my question. In your travels, did you come across a white cow wandering by itself? I've been searching for it all morning."

As though he could understand Begonia's question, the baby's eyes lit up, and he began to coo.

"I did, indeed, see a wandering white cow on our path through the pasture," the mother said. "I would guess it was two hours ago. A sweet thing, with a gentle nature, and a marking on the forehead that looked like a baby's bottom."

Begonia sighed. Speaking of babies' bottoms, there was no ignoring *this* baby's dampness now.

"Odd that you should say that." The voice came from behind Begonia. She turned to see a lanky woodsman with an ax slung over one shoulder striding along the other fork in the road, the one pointing toward the forest. "I saw a white cow this morning, too, heading through the woods. Nearer to my road than yours. About two hours ago. But the mark on its forehead was a tree stump. No doubt about it."

"Oh dear," moaned Begonia. "It's not possible! How could she be in two places at once?"

The mother rose to her feet, dusted herself off, and relieved Begonia of her soggy burden. "I don't know what you're saying, young lady," she said. "They have different markings. They must be different cows."

It would be hopeless to explain to the woman how Alfalfa's forehead mark seemed to look like whatever its beholder knew best, so Begonia didn't bother. Surely there was nothing magical about it. It was just people seeing what they wanted to see. Peony did it all the time.

"I'm only a poor widow," the mother said again, "but never let it be said that I failed to thank you for holding my baby. Here. Take this hairpin." She pulled a long pin from her hair and offered it to Begonia. In the process, strands of her hair came loose and tumbled down her neck very prettily.

Begonia had had a long day. She stared at the hairpin. She didn't even know how to do fancy things with her hair. Dairymaids had little occasion for anything more than braids.

"You never know when a particular hairpin may turn out to be just the hairpin you need. Here, woodsman." The mother turned toward the lanky man with his ax and bundle. "Our paths seem to be headed in the same direction for a spell. Meet my baby." And before the woodsman could say nay, she'd handed her infant to him.

A bewildered Begonia tucked the hairpin into her apron and watched as the travelers' two silhouettes got smaller and smaller. Just precisely, she thought, as her chances of ever finding her cow and returning home seemed to be doing.

6

A FINDER OF LOST THINGS, AND A BAFFLING MAP

Begonia stood at the fork in the road. She looked to the left, then to the right. Forest or field, woods or pasture. Tree stump or baby's bottom. Whatever should she do?

"Alfalfa!" she cried aloud. "Where *are* you?"

A rumpled head poked out from a thick, flowering bush that grew a ways back from where the two roads met.

"Is this 'Alfalfa' of yours an ancestor spirit?" the head's owner inquired.

Begonia backed away in astonishment. A talking bush! A rustling bush with purple blossoms and a human head. A bush with a head of messy hair, full of leaves and twigs.

"She must be, or why else would you summon her in this way? But it's customary to show more respect. Try 'Venerable

Grandmother,' perhaps, or 'Blessed Great-Auntie.' The dead still appreciate courtesy."

Begonia's throat was dry, and her feet were sore. Her cow was lost, and now she had lost her mind and saw visions of talkative shrubbery. Still, if she was already mad, she might as well carry on a conversation with this bush.

"Who in heaven's name has an ancestor spirit named 'Alfalfa?'" she demanded of the shrub. "Alfalfa's not dead. She's my cow. And she's lost."

The head in the bush rose, revealing a human neck and body attached in the usual fashion. It was a boy, perhaps a year or two older than Begonia, dressed in shabby clothes that had once been brightly colored, like a patchwork quilt, but now were faded. His face was dirty, and his nails an absolute fright.

"You aren't a talking shrubbery at all," Begonia observed.

"Never claimed to be." He brushed sticks and leaves off himself. "I'm Key, and I can help. I specialize in finding things that are lost. Now, where did you last put your cow?"

"*Put* her?"

"Put her," repeated the strange boy. "People put things places. They put lentils in the soup, and spectacles in their slippers, and money under their mattresses. Where did you put your cow?"

"She's not a missing thimble. She's an animal."

"Even animals are put places," Key said patiently. "Pirates

put parrots on their shoulders, and magicians put rabbits in hats. Monkeys, I am told . . ."

"In the barn!" cried Begonia to stop him from talking. "Last night, before bed, I led her in from the pasture and put her in the barn. But that scarcely matters, because I milked her this morning, and because many people have seen her roaming all over the countryside today. Have *you* seen a white cow with an odd marking on her forehead?"

"Don't change the subject." Key paced back and forth, scratching his chin and furrowing his brow as if in deep thought. He really did have a most ridiculous look. He was tall and lean, with a terrible slouch, and that head of hair bristling with blossoms and leaves.

"You put her in the barn," the boy said, as if he'd made a breakthrough. "What did you *say to her* at the time?"

Begonia threw up her hands. "Nothing! Why should I say something to her?"

Key shook a finger at Begonia. "Everyone talks to their animals."

She sighed. "I don't think I did. If I did, it wasn't much. Maybe something like, 'Good night, cow.'"

Key began to circle about Begonia as if examining her. "A cow with a broken heart," he said to himself. "A milkmaid who gives her cows the silent treatment. Or, if she speaks, won't even call them by their names. A cold 'cow this, cow that' from her unfeeling lips. The cow decides she can't live with such sorrow anymore, so she runs away with her loneliness, searching for a better friend."

Chrysanthemumsy had taught Begonia her manners well enough, but Key's pronouncement pushed Begonia too far.

"Now, you look here, you Key," she said. "That is the most ridiculous thing I've ever heard. It's rude, and it's ignorant. A cow with a broken heart? Absurd! Cows are more stomach than heart, and I treat our milkers just fine, thank you very much. Clearly, you've never tended cows. And you've got twigs in your hair."

Key squinted at Begonia. "One doesn't need cow experience to know what's what," he said loftily. "The heart yearns for what it yearns for. I am an expert in hearts, being a romantic, as I am. I have the soul of a poet."

Begonia would have no more of this. "You have the soul of an idiot." Every minute she spent talking to this irritating boy was a minute she couldn't afford. "Besides, I thought you were an expert at finding lost things."

Key crossed his arms across his chest and made a great show of not looking at Begonia. "I am a man of many talents." He sniffed.

"You are a *boy* of no knowledge where cows are concerned," Begonia informed him.

"So what?" Key shrugged. "My family is more in the pig line. Pigs have sensitive souls, I can assure you. Offending a pig puts it off its feed for at least three days. A true pig-man wouldn't dream of it."

Begonia stretched her last stretch and turned her face toward the grassy pastured fields. One road was probably as good as another, she reasoned, and it was time to get moving. "Goodbye," she told Key firmly. "You've been no help whatsoever, but it was good of you to want to try."

"Well, give a fellow a minute to get his things," protested Key. "It's no use you leaving in such a rush. I'll just have to chase after you, and it's hot enough already. I'll get sweaty."

Begonia halted in her tracks. "Who said anything about you coming along?"

Key disappeared into the bush and began tossing assorted objects over his shoulder: socks, a comb, a cup, a garlic clove. They flew up out of the bush like butterflies and fluttered to the ground.

"I told you," *fling*, "that I would help you find your cow," *fling*, "and the job's not finished yet."

"That's quite all right," Begonia said. "I can look for her by myself."

"Besides," *fling, fling*, "a romantic soul like mine couldn't possibly allow a damsel in distress to get away from him unhelped."

There was no point in encouraging this nuisance. Not another inch. Begonia marched resolutely down the grassy path to the right and called over her shoulder. "I'm not a damsel in distress!"

Footsteps on the path jogged after her. "Of course you are," came Key's panting voice. "Are you happy right now?"

"No!"

"See?" He caught up with her and hoisted a shabby gray sack over his shoulder. "You're distressed. And you're clearly a damsel. So you're a damsel in distress. As a romantic, I cannot leave you until you're happy. It's in our Code. The Code of the Romantics."

"The Code of the *what* . . ." Begonia halted. "Wait. You mean, when I'm happy, you'll leave?"

Key nodded. "In a very tragic fashion. That makes it all the more romantic."

Begonia bunched up her cheeks in the widest, most exaggerated smile she could produce. "*Tra-la-la,*" she sang brightly through her smile, swinging her skirts about while skipping down the road as her sister Peony would do. "*See how happy I am today! The sky is blue, the clouds are fluffy, and I haven't a care in the world!*"

Key folded his arms across his chest. "You wouldn't fool a pig with that performance," he observed, "though, to be fair, pigs aren't easily fooled." He picked up his pace. "No, my mind's made up. I'm here to help." He waggled a finger in her face. "The Code of the Romantics warns that some damsels may try to pretend they're not in distress, out of politeness, but a true romantic should help them anyway."

Begonia let her false smile melt. "I say your Code is selfish," she said. "I should be allowed to be unhappy if I want to be."

Key scratched his scalp, scattering kindling along their path. "You'll forgive me for saying so," he said, "but there's something wrong in your head. Who would ever want to be unhappy?"

Begonia quickened her pace. "You make me dizzy."

"Tsk, tsk," replied Key. "We might as well get acquainted. I can't leave until I've done at least one heroic deed for you, and from the looks of things, that could take a while. Now, what's your name?"

Begonia glanced at the sun, sailing steadily across the sky, and wondered how much daylight she had left to search for Alfalfa. This boy was harder to get rid of than an upset stomach. She sighed. "My name's Begonia."

Key's face lit up. "Begonia? A very romantic name."

She glared at him. "No, it isn't. It's absurd."

"I beg to differ. Well, Maid Begonia, where do you come from?"

"Two Windmills."

Key gazed at her in wonder. "You live inside two windmills? One of them for odd days, and the other one for evens?"

Odd days, indeed. This was the oddest day Begonia could remember. "It's the name of our village."

"Ah. A village with two windmills! It must be very prosperous."

Begonia scanned the hedgerows, searching for any trace of a white cow. "There's only one left, now."

"And I suppose changing the name of the village to Only One Windmill Now would seem rather embarrassing."

Begonia rolled her eyes. "I suppose."

"I can picture it," said Key, gesturing broadly. "A windmill. A farm. A barn. A cow. And you there, in your pink scarf, milking her."

"There's a little more to it than that," Begonia said. "Here. Let me show you." She reached into her pocket and pulled out the parchment scroll of the mapmaker's gift to her. She stopped to study it. "See, this is a map of our village. My home is . . ."

Key peered over her shoulder. "Your home is where?"

She looked at him in alarm. "Not there anymore!" She spread the map out wide. "This morning the map showed my house, my barn, all the neighbors' homes, and Two Windmills. But now it shows nothing of the kind! It's all strange territory I've never seen."

Key blinked at the map. "Perhaps you misread it before."

She shook her head. "I know my own home, don't I?"

"If you do, that makes you luckier than some."

Begonia stuffed the scroll back into her pocket and trudged along in deep gloom. Then Key's last words tickled her memory.

"Don't you know your home, Key?" she asked.

He scratched his nose. "I know it," he said at length, "better than it knows me. I intend to find a better one."

"Oh." Begonia wasn't sure what else to say. Leave home

to find a better one? Did young people actually do that? The thought had never occurred to her. Leave Mumsy? Leave Peony? . . . Begonia considered. She wouldn't want to leave Peony for good, she decided. Just for a day or two, here and there.

She gazed over at Key, walking beside her. It seemed to her that there was a story behind his cryptic words, but the chatty boy didn't seem to want to talk about it.

They walked for a while, but Key, it seemed, was not a person who could bear silence.

"Have you any family?"

Thinking again of Mumsy gave Begonia a pang of sadness. How her mother would worry when she didn't return home with Alfalfa by dark!

"A mother and a younger sister."

"A younger sister," echoed Key. "I always wished for a younger brother or sister. I myself am the youngest of a very large family."

Begonia pictured a family full of children who looked just like Key, twigs and blossoms and all. "How large a family?"

"No one is quite certain."

Begonia forgot Alfalfa for a moment. "You're joking!"

Key shook his head. "They would never hold still long enough for my parents to count."

"But . . . !"

"Twins, triplets, neighboring cousins . . . Once you have more children than fingers, and more piglets than children, what does it matter?" He sighed. "Tell me, does your younger sister look up to you? Admire your wisdom? Follow your example in all things?"

A picture of spoiled, smug Peony flashed in Begonia's brain. She let out a bitter laugh. "Hardly."

"Really?" Key picked a wild berry off a bush and offered it to Begonia. "I would've thought so."

"She tattles about me to Mumsy nonstop and says I do everything stupidly."

Key patted Begonia's shoulder. "I'm sure you don't do everything stupidly."

"Thanks."

They plodded along. Any other day, Begonia would have loved this long walk, reveling in the view around each new bend. The fields would have delighted her with their delicate green stalks of new vegetable plants rising up from the damp earth. These many-colored wildflowers, blooming in the hedgerows—on another day she would have picked a bouquet for Mumsy.

But today she could barely notice any of it. All she saw was what she didn't see. A cow.

"I've taken the wrong road," she said aloud. "I should've taken the forest path. That must be where Alfalfa has gone. Perhaps she's gone searching there for some shade." She pointed toward her left, where the forest made a dark border to the western horizon. "What if she's been eaten by a panther?"

"Let me see that map of yours again," said Key. He pored over the image, muttered to himself, looked about, then held the map up to show Begonia.

"Look. See there? The bush with the purple flowers? That's where I've been . . . where we met a short while ago. And this is the road we're on, and this one"—he traced his finger along the other fork in the road, the one headed due west that veered through the forest—"is the path we didn't take."

Begonia shook her head. "I still don't understand," she said. "This map showed my home and my village this morning. It showed none of this territory. I'm telling you, I saw it with my own eyes."

Key pursed his lips. "See that cottage up ahead, beyond the bend? There it is on the edge of the map."

"So?"

"So," he repeated, "it wasn't on the map half an hour ago, when you showed it to me the first time."

Begonia was unconvinced. "How can you be sure?"

"A Finder of Things That Are Lost," explained Key, with an air of injured dignity, "is also, conversely, and by extension, A Noticer of Things That Weren't There Before."

Begonia bit her lip. Could it be true? Should she believe this strange boy?

"But then," she whispered, "that can only mean that the map . . ."

"Changes?" supplied Key.

"Ink can't change!"

"Moves?" inquired Key.

"But how could it?"

Key shrugged. "There are forces at work in the world about which we know so very little."

"Would you please speak normally?" Begonia cried.

Key eyed her with a surprised expression. "All right then," he said simply. "Magic."

7

EMPTINESS, AND
PALACE PLOTTING

Late morning, in the palace.

Five days had passed since he'd vanished, and still the emperor had not returned. An eerie quiet settled over his elegant dwelling.

At first, all had been hustle and commotion in the hours after he disappeared. Searchers fanned out across the empire, hunting for their ruler, leaving the palace staff tense and watchful.

Meanwhile, servants who'd known the emperor since he was a boy on his mother's knee wept. The palace priest lit candles before the shrines of emperors and empresses past, praying that their great-great-however-many-greats-grandson would come home.

The old chancellor seemed to age ten years overnight. He'd served the royal family since the current emperor's grandfather had wielded the scepter, and he worked tirelessly now to find his missing young lord. In search of clues, he dispatched waves of diplomats on voyages to the halls of neighboring kingdoms to dance with the elegant ladies of those glittering courts. Was there a plot brewing? Had the emperor vanished at some king's wicked hand?

Many in the palace doubted the chancellor's strategy. No earthly power, they said, could've produced that scream of mortal terror, nor caused those doorknobs to burn. Nothing born this side of paradise, the kitchen staff whispered, could do it. But others said, as they so often did, that cooks and bakers were a superstitious set.

Neither the searchers nor the diplomats dared reveal what they were searching for, nor whom they hoped to find. The old chancellor warned the servants most urgently to be cautious and tell no one what had happened. No one must know that the emperor had vanished. For if the empire were to discover itself leaderless—if power-hungry monarchs from across the sea should discover that the great and wealthy empire of Camellion, that jewel of the Three Continents, that succulent peach dangling from the world's Tree of Paradise, lacked an emperor to command its armies—then who could say what might follow? Wars and intrigues. Anarchy and terror. The end of an ancient empire, and the plundering of its treasures.

Art galleries. Jewel-encrusted corridors. Carvings of rare and exquisite beauty. Pleasure boats and botanical gardens. What would become of it all? The Imperial Menagerie. Would its terrifying beasts be set loose to savage children in the streets?

These and other dismal thoughts were all that remained to occupy the minds of the army of servants who no longer had an emperor to please. On they worked, and scrubbed, and sewed, and baked, as though he were still home. When he did return, all must be ready. There was a birthday celebration to prepare for, after all. How their hearts would soar to hear the sounds of his complaints and demands once more! They didn't mind. It came with the job. Every job had its quirks. Scribes were squinty, bakers plump, harpists high-strung, and emperors domineering. Especially young ones. It was only because they were nervous. In time, they'd learn.

The Guards of the Imperial Bedchamber drooped at their posts. The royal confectioners baked tiny pastries out of pure habit, but their hearts weren't in it. The palace chefs set mousetraps and mourned over wilting lettuces the emperor would never eat. The Imperial Masseuse's hands grew stiff, and the Singers of Songs for the Evening Shift sang mournful dirges into brass pipes to which no one turned a listening ear.

The Keeper of the Imperial Aviary was the one person on the palace staff who wasn't worried about the emperor. He mourned his missing ostrich, a tall and handsome male the keeper had nicknamed Lightfoot. The emperor, as far as he was concerned, could look after himself, but who would take care of Lightfoot? Would rude boys try to pluck his fluffy wing feathers?

No, nothing was right anymore, reflected the butler, formerly the cupbearer's second assistant. In the five days since the emperor vanished, the butler had been kept busy serving beverages to other nobles in the palace. Three, to be precise: Count Rudo, the emperor's cunning cousin; Lord Hacheming, an aristocrat descended from the royal priestly line; and Duke Baxa the Ruthless, the son of a captain in the former emperor's army.

These three were the emperor's closest associates. Not friends, for this particular emperor didn't know the first thing about how to treat others in a friendly way. But he did have people willing to lose to him at games to relieve his boredom, people to complain to, or complain about, as the mood suited him. Rudo, Hacheming, and Baxa were the emperor's companions, and they lived in the palace. No one remembered their being invited. They appeared out of nowhere and made themselves comfortable, much as termites do. Each of them powerful, wealthy, and well-connected, they could be very dangerous to the emperor if they wished to be. They were among the first to hear of his disappearance. There could be no hiding the news from them.

The Imperial Butler entered the small salon where the three had gathered after a late breakfast that morning. He carried a decanter of wine and three gleaming golden cups inlaid with silver animal patterns, neatly arranged on a crystal tray. He bowed low, then began to pour.

". . . leadership was a disaster," murmured Count Rudo to the others. Sunlight gleamed off his glossy, oiled curls of jet-black hair and the solitary curl of his beard.

"Gone for days now," was bald, round Lord Hacheming's deep, bullfroggy reply. He was, indeed, an amphibious-looking person, with rolls of neck that might have been gills, wispy whiskers dangling below his otherwise smooth-shaven face, and bulging toad's eyes.

"Shh." Duke Baxa placed a finger over his lips and flicked his eyes, briefly, in the butler's direction. His thin mustache quivered like a flung dagger impaled in a door.

The butler poured out the last drop of Hacheming's wine without spilling a drop, all the while keeping his face as placid as a moonlit pond.

"That will be all." Duke Baxa waved a hand at the butler, who soundlessly left the room.

But he didn't like it. Something didn't feel right. So he did what he had never done before. He violated the sacred rules of buttling, rules drilled into him since he was a fifth assistant cupbearer. He lingered near the doorway, stilled his breath, and listened.

"There's no hint of a clue of him ever coming back." That would be Count Rudo, with a voice as oily as his hair. "I tell you, the longer you wait, the more your chances weaken. Someone else will take the throne." *Wait for what?*

The butler heard the sound of a heavy glass being set down on a wooden table. "Patience." Must be Baxa.

"What if he isn't dead?" said Hacheming. "Some servants believe he went mad. He could be roaming anywhere. Which means he could return."

"And how long do you think he'd survive as a madman roaming the countryside?" inquired Baxa. "No. We wait for the time to be right, and then we act. Our opening could come at any moment." A swallowing sound. "The empire needs a leader. A real one, not that doddering fossil of a chancellor. Soon I shall provide them such a leader. When I take the throne, you'll share the spoils."

Low chuckles, and the chiming sound of golden glasses clinking. The butler's breath caught in his throat.

"Hsst! Did you hear that?"

The butler backed away as quickly as he dared, keeping his eyes on the door. Rudo's shining hair poked out the doorway just as the butler ducked around a corner.

Safe, the butler thought. *For now.*

8

A CHOOSY CAT,
AND A HORRID BEAST

BEGONIA MARCHED ALONG THE ROAD, fuming. She paused every dozen steps or so and consulted the map. She frowned and marched some more. She didn't want to believe it. She longed to deny it. But she couldn't.

The map was moving. The face of the drawing, ever so slightly, almost imperceptibly, changed.

She watched over a long stretch of walking as an innocent-looking boulder slid slowly off the edge of the page and vanished. She remembered passing it hours back.

"There's no such thing as magic!" she fumed.

Key shrugged. "Suit yourself."

"Those are children's tales," she said. "People talk about magic, but that's just old-timey stuff."

"Undoubtedly."

"Oh, would you stop that?"

Key spread his hands out wide. "We've established the fact that the map is moving, a thing which we know to be impossible. What other explanation is there?"

"There must be one," Begonia insisted, "that we haven't found yet."

"Maybe an ancestor spirit is moving it," Key said.

Begonia glared at him. "Nobody really believes that, either."

Key halted in his tracks and gaped at her. "You don't believe in ancestors?"

How, Begonia wondered, did she find herself trapped in a day where this odd boy interrogated her relentlessly?

"Of course I do," she said. "I believe they lived and died. I believe we owe them great honor and gratitude. We celebrate them in lots of ways. With rituals. And, you know, just with how we live." She paused to think. What *did* she really believe, come to think of it?

"And maybe," she went on, "for all I know, maybe they do really watch us from . . . wherever they are. If they're anywhere. But they're gone, don't you see?" She looked to see if Key did see, but if he did, he wasn't letting on. "The idea of ancestors *doing something*, something real in the world, is just a bunch of stories."

Key's expression bespoke concern for Begonia, and pity, as if she had a serious disease, or maybe a smut dangling from her nose. "What about demons, then?"

"That's different," she said. "Who else steals eggs from

the coop before I find them? Demons aren't magic. They're just . . . demons."

Key gave her a strange look. "Obviously." He'd been shedding leaves and twigs for miles, yet still seemed to have as many in his hair as at first. He pointed to the map in Begonia's hand. "Do you think demons are working that map?"

"But that would mean Master Mapmaker is a sorcerer," she protested. "I've known him for years. He's always there, with his funny spectacles and pens, just scratching away."

Key shrugged. "And yet he gave you a map that moves."

"If only it could move to the spot where Alfalfa is." Begonia began to stuff the map back into her pocket, then paused. "Map," she told it loudly, "can you show me where my cow Alfalfa is?"

The paper did nothing.

"Mark the path that leads to my cow?"

Still nothing. Not so much as a parchment corner rustling in the breeze. So Begonia moved on, heavy in foot and in heart.

"I would just like to point out," said Key, "that you don't believe in ancestors or magic, and you don't believe this is the work of demons, yet you're begging a piece of parchment to help you."

She glowered at Key. "Perhaps I am becoming more open to possibilities."

"Perhaps you don't speak its language," Key offered.

"You're no help."

"You pierce my heart," said Key. "A romantic lives for nothing but to be helpful."

The sun began to sink in the west. Its orange rays blinded them as they walked along, heading straight into its burning fire. Begonia wrapped her pink scarf loosely over her forehead and eyes and kept her view fixed on the path beneath her feet. She should've turned and gone home long before this, but it always seemed as though Alfalfa must be just around the next bend. One bend led to another, and now the day was gone. Where would she sleep? She'd never in her life slept away from home. How Mumsy would worry! She was miles from Two Windmills, all alone, save for this curious Key, and she might fall prey to who-knew-what? Panthers? Thieves? Demons that stalked the roads by night? Demons or no, desperate criminals or no, Begonia had overheard enough of the bedtime stories Mumsy always read Peony to know that tucked into bed at home, after dark, is where a girl should always stay.

Up ahead, they heard a rumbling sound, and with it a yowling screech, as though a thousand demons sang together.

Begonia gasped and hurried off the road into the tall grasses.

"What are you doing?" Key called after her.

"Shh!" she hissed, and waved at him frantically to get off the path. "Listen to that horrible sound!"

Key watched the road ahead for what felt like an eternity, then joined Begonia.

"It's a wagon," said Key, "carrying a tall cage. Whatever's inside, it's making an awful racket."

The tall, tottering vehicle rumbled along, swaying and glowing from the setting sun. As it approached, it revealed its cargo: angry cats. Dozens of them.

The screeching and screaming only grew louder as the wagon approached. The horse, a sturdy fellow, snorted and tossed its head about frantically, showing the whites of his eyes. The driver sat hunched in misery on the seat-board. He wore a scarf tied twice around his head, and, still, he pressed his hands to his ears and moaned.

"The poor horse," Begonia said. "That sound would make anyone lose their sanity." She rose and hurried after the wagon, then jogged to keep up with the driver.

"Excuse me," she cried over the chorus of cats. "Have you seen a wandering white cow as you traveled this way?"

The driver kept his hands clamped to the sides of his head and ignored Begonia.

She watched the kitties through the slats of the cage walls. They arched their backs and clawed at their prison bars. They trod on top of one another in their eagerness to get free. Their paws jabbed through holes in the cage and groped at empty air.

"Poor things," said Begonia. "I wonder what happened to them. I wish we could help."

One fluffy gray cat, she noticed, made no commotion. It sat calmly in the back corner, watching Begonia with gold eyes. As the wagon rumbled on, eastward, toward where Begonia and Key had come from, this cat poked a white paw out. It swatted at the latch holding the cage together and, with a few quick jabs, released the lock. The door swung open, and an avalanche of hissing, yowling kitties came pouring out.

They hit the ground and scattered, disappearing in a flash in every direction. Only one cat remained in the wagon—the gray one with the golden eyes. It sat neatly with its tail wrapped around its paws and waited.

The driver called to the horse to stop, then jumped down from his seat. At the sight of the (almost) empty wagon, he fell to his knees and tore at his hair.

"Whoever sent him on this errand won't be very happy with him now, I suppose," Begonia whispered. "I hope those poor kitties can find a safe place to sleep. And a nice bowl of milk."

The driver quickly unhitched the horse from the wagon. He climbed onto the horse's back, and together they took off at a run.

"He's wearing the tunic of an imperial servant," said Key. "He must have come from the palace, from the emperor. The emperor doesn't look kindly on servants who don't complete their tasks. That driver'll need to flee Camellion now if he wants to avoid the dungeons."

They rose from their hiding place and approached the stranded wagon. At the sight of them, the gray kitty jumped gracefully down from the wagon bed and rubbed against both their ankles. Begonia bent down to pet her soft fur. The cat allowed the petting for a moment, then leaped up onto her shoulder and began deeply sniffing Begonia's hair.

Key's jaw dropped. "What in the name of the emperor is she doing?"

"Biting my hair," replied Begonia. The kitty had begun to slide her teeth along her scalp, sniffling and chewing lovingly at her hair. It tickled.

"But *why?*"

"There's no explaining cats," Begonia said. "Never mind. She's not hurting me."

"Shoo, cat! Shoo!" Key waved his hands at the kitty.

Begonia backed away. "Leave her alone," she said. "She likes me."

"Likes you like I like my dinner," muttered Key. "She wants to *eat* you."

"Just my hair."

"Oh, well, then. Just your hair." Key rolled his eyes and moved on.

"Cats have always liked me." Begonia followed after him, trying not to drop her furry stowaway. "It drives my sister, Peony, batty that our kitty, Catnip, prefers me to her. Ow! Claws!"

They continued their march toward the sinking sun, and the cat settled down comfortably on Begonia's shoulder, with her soft bulk pressing against her neck. Spending the night alone and outdoors felt slightly less terrifying now with this purring new friend.

Begonia pulled the map from her pocket once more. "We need to find a place to sleep," she said. "We're running out of daylight." She held the map where the sun's rays could hit it. It seemed that they were more or less always at the center of the map. She studied the other details. Roads, shrubs, a stream.

"Key! Is this the spot where I met you?" She pointed to the purple shrub, which was now at the very bottom of the map.

Key nodded. "So what?"

Begonia pointed to the two roads that forked out from that spot. "Look. This is the pasture road we took, and this is the forest road we didn't take." She gestured up higher on the map. "That looks like a stream, and it cuts across both roads. We've seen no sign of Alfalfa, so my guess is she never came this way. When we come to the stream, we could follow it to reach the forest road. Maybe we'll find her there."

"I could use something to drink," said Key.

"Alfalfa's probably thirsty, too," said Begonia. "Come on! Maybe we'll find her at last."

They picked up their pace and hurried onward. The sun dipped below the horizon, leaving the sky soft and golden and streaked with pink, though Begonia knew it couldn't last long. Soon the lingering light in the sky would be gone.

"Key," Begonia asked, "is 'Key' the name your parents gave you?"

They covered long strides of ground until Begonia wondered if he'd heard the question at all, before Key finally answered.

"Eventually, I think," he said. "Or else my older sisters and brothers gave me the name. They often said that I was fond of playing with keys when I was very young. And I like to tinker with locks."

"What do you mean, 'eventually'?" demanded Begonia. She pushed the gray cat's flicking tail out of her face.

Key bent down to remove a shoe and shook a pebble out of it, hopping along on one foot in a most absurd fashion. "My parents and my relatives," *hop, hop,* "weren't the sort to name a baby." *Hop.* "They don't name pigs, either. It makes it harder to sell them. But we children gave one another nicknames sooner or later. I have a sister we call Mirror because she's so vain." He waved his shoe in the air. "I even have a cousin named Shoe because all he ever wanted was fancy shoes without farm muck on them." He glanced sideways at Begonia. "The one to really feel sorry for is my brother Spit."

Begonia didn't know what to say. How horrible!

"I always thought Mumsy was strange for naming us after flowers," she said. She glanced at her traveling companion and realized how little she knew about him.

"You said earlier," she said at length, "that you'd left home to search for a better one. What does that mean?"

"Why, to seek my fortune, of course," said Key. "Don't you

know young people who leave home in search of their fortune?"

"Not really, no."

Key deflated somewhat. "Neither do I. Perhaps it's going out of style." He pulled his shoe back on. "I'm beginning to question whether there really is a fortune out there with my name on it. I've looked under every rock, every fallen log, every shrub and tree."

"That would explain the twigs and leaves in your hair," muttered Begonia.

"The what in my hair?"

"Never mind." She shifted the cat to her other shoulder. "Why did you really leave home, Key?"

He gave her a long look. "One day I decided I'd hide in the pig barn and wait to see how long it would take for someone to notice I was gone."

Begonia's heart sank. She feared to hear what happened next.

"They never noticed," Key said. "After ten days, I left."

"*Ten days!*" Begonia gasped. "My Mumsy would come hunting for me if she couldn't find me after, oh, a few hours at most." Was Mumsy looking for her now?

Key patted her shoulder. "Well, as I said, that makes you lucky."

"What did you eat for ten days while you hid in the barn?"

Key shrugged. "Pig slop. I was used to it."

Begonia shuddered. She studied her traveling companion

out of the corner of one eye. He was the oddest boy she'd ever met, sticky as pine sap, and harder to get rid of than an infestation of fleas, but she couldn't help but feel sorry for him.

The song of water burbling over smooth stones reached their ears, and then the fresh, damp smell of well-watered grasses. They pushed their tired feet onward until, at last, they saw it up ahead—a dark stripe of land, with bushes and trees growing close by. A footbridge in the road arched over the stream while flecks of lavender sky rippled across its surface.

The kitty leaped off Begonia's shoulder and reached the water in one jump, where it began lapping for dear life. Key did likewise, plunging his face right into the stream. Perhaps he was unaware that his derriere revealed a hole or two in the bottom of his pants. Begonia knelt by the water and drank from her hand.

They drank as though they'd crossed a desert. They drank till their teeth hurt and their bellies ached. Water made Begonia forget everything else. Finally, she began to feel water-woozy, and she sat up and looked around. The sky to the east was fully dark now, and the last bits of gold in the west hung low on the horizon.

"Key," she called to the bottoms-up boy, who still drank like a camel. "It's nearly dark. We've got to get off this road and find a place to sleep."

Key's dripping head rose from the river. Twigs and leaves still protruded from his now-sopping hair. In the dim light, he looked like a young and scrawny version of a river god.

"You're right." He clambered to his feet, and together they picked their way through the grasses and rocks, following the creek toward the woods and the road they hadn't taken. The cool, damp water that had felt so refreshing after their hot march now chilled Begonia. Spring nights were still cold, and she had no blanket. What kind of night would this be?

The sky grew darker by the minute, and with the darkness came birdcalls and stirrings in grasses of the citizens of the night—animals unseen, with gruesome little snouts and claws. Bats swished and swooped overhead, and insects buzzed in Begonia's ears. The cat curled once more against her and buried its whiskery face in Begonia's neck. They reached the forest's edge and almost hesitated, but, keeping close to the stream, they pressed on.

Then Begonia saw it. In the dim forest shadows, some distance up ahead, and not far from the stream. Something white moved among the grasses.

"Key, look!" Begonia whispered. "Do you see it?"

Key squinted at the dark. It was only a narrow bit of white, and gray at that in the dimness, but he saw it, too.

"Your cow?" he asked.

"Shh." Begonia nodded. "It must be."

They crouched low in the undergrowth and crept forward softly. After all this walking, Begonia had no wish to give chase, and Alfalfa, she knew, could be fast when she wanted to be. Hadn't she already outstripped Begonia across the entire countryside?

They were close now. They could no longer see Alfalfa through the bushes, but they could hear her breathing.

"You go that way," Begonia whispered, pointing to the right, "and I'll take this side. On the count of three, we move in quickly."

Key agreed. He moved off a few paces.

"One," Begonia breathed, "two, three!"

They burst through the undergrowth.

There was no cow. There was—what was it?

Gloom and shadows, then her eyes adjusted. The kitty screeched and dug her claws into Begonia's shoulder. The shock of what they saw would return to haunt Begonia's nightmares long afterward.

A snake. A huge, long snake, straight upright, as tall as Begonia herself. Poised to attack, hissing and darting and weaving back and forth. With enormous eyes glinting in the darkness, and a snout like a bird's beak.

No. It *was* a bird's beak. Not a snake's head. That hideous, long white thing was a neck! A horrid, ropy neck.

Attached to the neck, on the ground, lay an enormous mass. A dark body. A bird body. And curled beside it lay a small human form, dressed in dirty pajamas.

Then the bird body rose, terrifyingly. A giant, a monster! It mounted up on gawky, mighty, scraggly legs and bolted toward them, flapping its powerful wings wide enough to knock Key and Begonia flat onto their backs.

Begonia lay gasping on the ground. Would the monster return? Was Key all right? Where had the kitty gone?

A thin, nasal voice rose from the ground. "Wretched peasant! You've scared off my ostrich. He's probably a mile away by now, and you'd better bring him back!"

9

A NIGHTTIME KNOCK,
AND A MOTHER'S DILEMMA

THERE WAS A SLOW KNOCK AT THE DOOR. A log settled in the fireplace, and Catnip, the yellow cat, yawned with all her fangs.

Peony, who had been allowed, under the circumstances, to stay up much past her bedtime, looked anxiously at the shadows on her mother's face.

"Is it Begonia, Mumsy?" she whispered.

"Shh." Chrysanthemumsy rose and wrapped her shawl around her throat. "You stay here."

She wanted desperately for it to be Begonia, but if it were her daughter, gone all day in search of a runaway cow, why would she knock? Why would she not burst right in to her own home, where her plate of dinner still sat warming by the fire, and the teakettle sputtered in anticipation? A knocking visitor . . . Chrysanthemumsy had raised the alarm of Begonia's absence throughout Two Windmills, so any visitor might bring welcome news. Still, she couldn't bear to imagine the reasons someone might knock at this hour, on this night.

She opened the door.

It wasn't her daughter. Of course it was not.

"Good evening, dearie."

"Madame Mustard-maker!" Mumsy tried to control the surprise in her voice. "You honor our home. Won't you come in? Have a cup of tea?"

Madame Mustard-maker stepped into the light spilling from the doorway. "Tea would be divine, dearie, but I'm afraid I haven't got time. Too much to poke around in, to stir up, to sniff. My, er, mustard, you know. Needs tending at the oddest hours."

Oh, please, Chrysanthemumsy thought, *get quickly to the point. Do you know something about my daughter?* She filled her lungs with air and held it there.

Madame Mustard-maker's eyes crinkled kindly. She patted Chrysanthemumsy's cheek. "Your daughter is safe, dearie. She's walked all day in search of your missing cow. Cows can be such impish things! I had a cow once who . . . never mind. Your Begonia is far from home, but she's well."

Chrysanthemumsy seized her hand. "How do you know?" She felt herself grow weak and shaky. "If she's far away, how could you possibly know?"

Madame Mustard-maker smiled. "You'll have to trust me. I'll look after her myself."

"But you're here," Mumsy said, "and she's far away. Or so you said."

"Oops!" Madame Mustard-maker patted her fingers playfully over her lips. "I'm always saying the wrong thing. Well, you'll have to trust me there, too. Near or far, I'll look after her."

Villagers had long said Madame Mustard-maker was odd, eccentric even, but never before had Chrysanthemumsy thought she might be truly mad. Certainly not dangerous.

"Have you taken my daughter somewhere?" Mumsy demanded.

"Mercy me!" cried the mustard-maker. "I? Take the flower girl somewhere? How could I? I weigh less than a partridge. She said *you* sent her in search of the lost cow."

Chrysanthemumsy let out her breath. Of course the tiny, ancient mustard-maker couldn't have taken Begonia anywhere. All this nonsense was the babble of an old woman who was slowly losing her wits. She should ignore it all.

But hope refused to die so easily. "If you know where she is, good mother," said Chrysanthemumsy, "won't you take me to her?"

Madame Mustard-maker's eyes softened. "It's been a long time," she said, "but a mother never forgets how it feels to worry for her children. Not tonight, dearie." She patted Chrysanthemumsy's arm. "I can't take you there tonight. But tomorrow is always full of possibilities. Take heart. Get some rest. Begonia is safe tonight. Please believe me."

And why should I believe you? Chrysanthemumsy wanted to say. *Why should I not be more terrified than ever by your cryptic message?*

But Madame Mustard-maker's eyes were kind. They didn't seem like the eyes of a madwoman. Chrysanthemumsy didn't dare take comfort from them, though the concern shining there seemed real.

"It appears I have no choice but to believe you," Chrysanthemumsy told her. She bowed. "Thank you for bringing me word."

10

A RUDE ENCOUNTER,
AND NOCTURNAL TERRORS

"FETCH ME MY BIRD, AND SEE TO MY DINNER," said the thin voice from the darkness.

It was the figure in pajamas, now risen and standing, who issued the orders.

Begonia climbed to her feet. "Who are you?"

"That is not your concern," the person said. "Find my bird, I said, and then bring me something to eat."

His voice buzzed like a mosquito in Begonia's ear. Mentally, she swatted it away. "Key," she called, "are you all right?"

"No, I am not all right," came the irritable voice again. "And my name is not 'key.' I'm famished. I've been wandering for days and reduced to *asking* rude persons for food. Asking! I said, bring me some—"

"Not *you*," said Begonia. "Key."

"I don't care a fig if you've lost your key," said the voice. "Fetch my bird and a bite to eat!"

Begonia's patience was wearing thin. "Not *my* Key," she said, "and not my *key*."

The owner of the strange voice sniffed. "You're raving mad."

"Key?" she cried. "Key?" She groped through the dark brambles in the direction she thought he'd gone, until finally she trod on something that wasn't ground.

"*Oof!*"

She grinned. Key, she considered, was probably not grinning.

"*Eee-yah!*" yelped the strange voice. The short, pajama-clad blur in the darkness clambered up a tree trunk. "Wh-who's there?"

"There you are." Begonia took Key's outstretched hand. "Why didn't you answer me?"

"What? Where am I?"

It was Key's voice, but it didn't sound like him. Begonia pulled him to a standing position. "Did you hit your head? Are you hurt?"

Key wobbled on his feet. "That thing," he moaned. "That monster . . . it struck me with its ferocious claws and sent me flying! It flung me across the forest!"

"Well, sort of," she said. "What's your name?"

"Key," he answered. "Don't you know me?"

"You know this intruder?" demanded the panicked voice of the stranger. "Drop your weapons! State your purpose!"

"Key has no weapons," Begonia told the voice. "Nor any purpose."

"Thanks a lot," muttered Key.

She ignored it. "Now, Key, what's my name?"

"Your names are completely unimportant!" shrilled the pajama-clad stranger from up in the tree. "Fetch me my ostrich and my supper!"

"Oh, is there supper?" asked Key.

"No."

"Oh. What's an ostrich? Is it supper?"

"The monster that knocked us over, I think," said Begonia. "Some sort of giant bird. I've heard of them, once, in a story. But *what is my name?*"

"This is terrible!" cried Key. "Has the monster made you forget your name?"

Begonia resisted the urge to grab him by his ears.

"I know my name," she said slowly. "I am trying to figure out if *you* know my name."

"Why, you're Begonia, of course," said Key, patting her on the head. "The funny girl with the pink scarf in her hair and the missing cow. The damsel I've chosen to rescue, romantically."

Begonia sighed with relief. She almost hugged him. If Key had been truly injured and lost his wits completely, what could she have done to help him, so far away from any town or city? But he was still himself. And just as determined as ever.

"Will you please leave off with this rescue nonsense?" she said.

"You won't call it nonsense when I dramatically rescue you."

In the distance, a wild animal's hunting cry ripped through the forest. Night was fully dark, now, and the biting wind was cold. Begonia's skin prickled while her heart sank.

The kitty meowed against her ankles. She scooped her into her arms and felt the soothing warmth of fur against her skin.

"Come on, Key," she said. "Grab your things. We'd better be moving on. Alfalfa's not here, so there's no reason why we should stay here and trouble this—person—anymore." She'd hesitated. She wasn't sure what sort of person she was dealing with. Man or woman, young or old, she didn't know about the stranger. All she knew was that he—or she—was unpleasant, rude, and accompanied by a monster bird that might, in all likelihood, come back.

"You can't leave me here," came the thin voice yet again. "I forbid it. Eek! Did you hear that?"

Begonia listened. "*That* was nothing more than a warbler's evening song. Haven't you ever been outside at night?"

"Don't be impertinent, little girl. I've been to many lawn parties that extended past sunset."

"Oh, well, then." Begonia was glad the darkness hid her face. "Sir," she said, cautiously, for she decided the voice was most likely male, "have you come across a white cow in your travels today?"

"Infernal thing wouldn't leave us alone," replied the apparently "sir" figure. "Plodded along beside us all afternoon, mooing at us, and playing games with my ostrich. Highly disrespectful and most inconvenient. I shall have it slaughtered and eaten for dinner."

"Oh, no!" Begonia cried. "You can't! That's my cow. You haven't already, er, eaten her, have you?"

"What am I, a butcher?" cried the voice. His tree was close by, but they could no more see him in the darkness than they could see Alfalfa.

Key chimed in. "Perhaps," he said. "Some of the nicest people I know are butchers. But you don't seem like any of the nicest people I know. What are you?"

The voice from the darkness sniffed. "What I am is not your concern."

"All right," said Key. "Where do you come from?"

"Shan't tell *you*."

"What's your name, then?"

The voice hesitated. "Names are unimportant for someone such as myself."

"You don't know your own name!" Begonia cried, disbelieving. "You actually don't know it!"

"I could have you imprisoned in the dungeons for such

disrespect," came the voice. "Without food or water. With rats snapping at your ankles."

Begonia turned away from the unpleasant figure. "Come on, Key, let's get going. We're wasting our time here. Alfalfa must be close by if she's stayed so close to this ostrich all afternoon. Though why she'd do that, I can't imagine."

"Shh! You shall not leave," the odious person hissed from his perch. "I command you to stay. After you retrieve my ostrich and fetch me something to eat."

Begonia had endured a long and trying day, and this troublesome person was becoming one problem too many. "Look, No-name," she said, "even if we had food to give you, we wouldn't share it after how rude you've been. And we haven't a crumb between us. Nor can we catch your bird. We'd have to be owls to see him in the dark. And horses to go fast enough to outrun him. It's just not possible. So I think you should stop giving orders."

"Stay," barked the man, "or face the consequences."

"Why? So you can insult us all night long? No, thank you. We'll find another place to sleep. You can find some other people to pick on if you like." Begonia began tugging Key toward the stream, but Key stayed still.

"Just out of curiosity," he ventured, "what consequences?"

Begonia had no patience for this delay. She pressed through the brambles until the throat-clenching, hair-raising cry of a forest animal rent the air. And a second, joining the first.

Begonia knew that cry.

It had made their cows' eyes roll white with terror when it came too near Two Windmills once before.

It had taken all the village huntsmen to drive it back to the wilds from whence it came.

But not before it got away with two of Grandmother Flummox's sheep.

"The panthers," said the man, "with bloodred eyes, and razor claws, that infest the forest, and hunt for food by night."

He began climbing higher up his tree branch with a speed Begonia wouldn't have expected of him. She herself could barely move for terror.

"You'd better climb, too, if you want to stay alive," he called down to them. "Not that tree! This one!"

"You first," said Key. "Hurry!"

It wasn't easy climbing in the dark. More than once, Begonia's foot slipped off a branch and nearly left her dangling. Then the panther's scream reached their ears again, closer this time. She gritted her teeth and climbed, with Key close behind. The gray kitty leaped past them up the trunk and into the high branches with incredible speed.

"Are you all right?" Key asked Begonia. "Got a good grip on the trunk?"

"Quiet!" whispered the stranger. "You're letting the panthers know where we are."

"They already do," Begonia whispered. "Look."

Only a glimmer of light from the low-rising moon penetrated the forest branches, but in its faint glow, as they held their breath, they saw shadows circling the tree. Shadows, with rippling muscles, long black tails, hungry red eyes, and wicked yellow teeth. And claws that raked the tree trunk, probing for the best way to begin their climb.

11

WHAT A PELICAN OUGHT
TO HAVE REALIZED

FARTHER ALONG IN THE FOREST, NEAR THE winding stream, a tree shuddered under the burden of an entire colony of nesting pink-backed pelicans, large birds with impressive wingspans and vast, pouchy beaks for catching fish. The weight of a dozen heavy nests, laden with eggs and nesting mothers, made the tree creak and moan in the night winds.

One such mother, roosting upon her nest, sighed in her sleep. A warm, soothing sensation had crept into her dreams. She would have smiled, but that's hard to do with a beak. She didn't know it, but the form of an old man had appeared in the branches of the heavy-laden tree. He hovered there, gently stroking the pelican's pinkish-gray back feathers.

"A *mapmaker*?"

The voice at his ear made the hovering man jump. The

pelican, paddling in the shallows of dream waters as a chick at her own mother's side, stirred as if a cold wind had brought wafting in the scent of a hunting stink-badger.

"Mr. I'm-So-Important-That-I-Deserve-to-Fiddle-with-Destiny takes on the appearance of a village *mapmaker*?"

"Hush!" the old man whispered. "You'll wake Mama Pelican."

"Leave her out of it," said the newcomer, the hovering form of an older woman. "Leave off with your bad impersonation of that nice old man. And leave my Begonia to me."

"You're one to talk." He brushed his fingertips over the pelican's crown feathers. Her funny-lidded eyes stirred. "A mustard-maker? It figures you'd do something ridiculous."

The old woman tossed a flap of her shawl over her shoulder.

"I wouldn't have had to become the mustard-maker if you hadn't up and decided to be the mapmaker," she said. "What did you mean by it? Giving my girl a magic map? She'll never know what to think of the real mapmaker again. I gave her one specific job to do, but now her head's so turned around she doesn't know which way is up."

The old man glanced at the old woman. "Neither do you, apparently."

In all her scolding, the grandmother spirit hadn't realized that she'd been rotating in midair until she practically floated sideways. She righted herself abruptly. "Explain yourself."

The grandfather spirit stroked the pelican mother and soothed her dreams until even the growing chicks inside the eggs felt happy waves of warm contentment.

"I gave her the map," he said, "to help her find her way, whatever befalls her. It's been my observation that the people *you* meddle with need all the help they can get."

She folded her arms across her chest. "You do your *own* meddling," she told him. "Don't you meddle in *my* meddling with *your* meddling. It isn't sporting."

"If I ever figure out what that means . . ."

"You just tend to your emperor," the grandmother spirit said briskly, "and leave my Begonia to me." She vanished in a puff.

The grandfather spirit stroked the mother pelican again before fading into the darkness. She slumbered on, lulled by memories of her mama bird and drowsy dreams of her own downy chicks to come, which she would gather safely under her far-reaching wings.

12

MOUNTING PERIL,
AND UNLIKELY HELP

HOW WOULD IT FEEL, TO WAIT TO DIE?
Like this?

What was strange was the quiet. They clung to their perches, the three of them: Begonia, the stranger, and Key, not daring to breathe. The moon mounted the dome of the sky, rising over the treetops to cast its cold beams down upon the glossy hides of their impending doom.

One panther circled the tree trunk. The other stood on its hind legs and spread its forelegs wide around the tree. It looked for all the world like a hug. A hug from a cat that was huge and black, with murderous red eyes.

And all the time in the world.

The hugging panther chose each hold slowly, carefully. It flexed its muscles without a care.

Then it jumped. It still clung to the tree trunk, but it had now cut the distance between the ground and Key in half.

Key yelped in terror. "Shoo! Shoo!"

"'Shoo, shoo'? Is that the best you can do?" the stranger called from the top of the tree. "Throw something at the demon cat!"

"Throw what?" cried Begonia. "You, perhaps? Key, here, take my hand!"

"You can't throw me," the stranger said. "I'm too important."

The panther leaped again, only barely missing Key's foot as Begonia pulled him up higher.

"We'll never make it," cried Begonia. "We're climbing for dear life, but the wicked beast isn't even trying!"

Overhead, from up in the thin branches, her terrified little gray kitty yowled.

"Never surrender, Maid Begonia," gasped Key. "We're not defeated yet."

"Two panthers, two children," said the stranger in the tree. "One for each. I'm higher than you, so I should be all right. But this is highly upsetting. I dislike messy things."

"Be *quiet!*"

The panther coiled its muscles for a last and deadly leap. Then it paused, and turned.

The panther on the ground heard it, too. A growl rumbled in its throat. In the distance, they heard something tearing rapidly through the forest.

A milk cow's moo reached Begonia's ears.

"*Alfalfa?*"

As smoothly as it had scaled the tree, the climbing panther peeled itself off the tree trunk in a noiseless pounce back to the forest floor. Together, the two panthers padded off in the direction of the moo.

Begonia shook with relief. But the danger wasn't for away, and now it was chasing her cow. "Poor Alfalfa!" She whispered. "Have we come all this way only to hear her be killed by vicious panthers?"

"We will remember her with gratitude," Key said, panting, "and honor. But I can't exactly be sorry that it's her they're chasing, and not us."

They heard more panther screams, and Begonia wished she could plug her ears, but she needed her hands to keep her grip.

Noises in the distance came nearer, and again they heard a hunter cat's cry.

Then a panther's dark shape sprinted underneath their perch, retreating in the opposite direction. Its mate came after, yowling as the huge monster bird chased it, dealing a massive kick with its long legs that sent the panther flying.

The three creatures disappeared into the forest. The sound of their chase gradually faded away.

"Did I see what I thought I saw?" Begonia wondered aloud. "Were two deadly panthers just chased away by *a bird?*"

As she spoke, the gray kitty found Begonia's shoulder and

climbed on. The poor trembling kitty's tail was thick as a small tree limb.

"I knew my ostrich would protect me," the smug stranger said. "Now, help me down. We can't stay up here all night like monkeys."

"Help yourself down," snapped Begonia. "You were awfully cheery about watching us die first." She began the dangerous work of descending the tree in the dark.

"I rescued you!" cried the repulsive man.

Key laughed bitterly. "Not even close. Your bird did."

The stranger shook his tree branch. Begonia held on for dear life, and thought of Peony's spoiled fits. "I'm allowed to take credit for what my servants do. Always. My pets, too."

"Maybe you do that in your little world," Begonia said. "But here in the real world, we prefer the truth."

They reached the ground and sank to their trembling knees. Then they rolled onto their sides and dissolved into the soil on the forest floor.

"Think those panthers will come back?" Key asked Begonia.

The shock of what had just happened—and what had nearly happened—caught up to Begonia then. She'd nearly died! A horrible, terrifying, excruciating death! She clutched her arms tightly around her sides. She couldn't answer Key. She turned away to hide the tears running down her cheeks and the shuddering in her breath.

But Key had heard her. For once the boy didn't know what to say. He placed a hand on her shoulder and kept it there.

Begonia wiped her cheeks with a sleeve and drew a deep breath.

"I don't know if they'll come back," she said at last. "I hope not. I hope the ostrich scared them. Our best hope is to stay close tonight and get whatever sleep we can. Tomorrow morning, cow or no cow, I'm going home."

13

MORE DARK DEEDS ON THAT FATEFUL NIGHT

MIDNIGHT, IN THE PALACE.

Servants and staff had long since gone to sleep, all except for those whose mission it was to pass the nighttime hours wide awake, keeping watch. With no emperor to protect, the night watchmen drooped at their posts, but of course the palace, which was the seat of government, must still be patrolled.

The Imperial Butler was not one of those whose job it was to keep a lonely nighttime vigil. He ought to have been deep in slumber, but he lay, this cool spring night, tossing fitfully between his sheets as sleep was snatched from him by curious dreams. He heard noises and footsteps. He imagined he heard the emperor's voice summoning him for a drink.

He brooded. Could the emperor have returned? Might someone else want a beverage? Perhaps the chancellor was having trouble sleeping and needed some warm milk. Or perhaps those three companions of the emperor's were up to some trouble. A dark thought, indeed. They'd been acting stealthy and secretive all day—all week, come to think of it—and the Imperial Butler didn't like the piercing stare each of them gave him whenever he passed by. Did they suspect he had heard their plans that morning?

He rose and dressed. Sleep was impossible now, so he might as well explore the nighttime corridors. It couldn't do any harm.

No one knew better than the Imperial Butler how to creep like a cat through the carpeted halls. It was part of his buttling training. Carrying a small, shaded oil lamp, he made his rounds, nodding to the guards stationed even now outside the emperor's lonely bedchamber. He paused to listen at servants' and courtiers' bedroom doors, waiting for any sound of someone in need or distress. But all slept, it seemed. Only he had been plagued by restless dreams.

He turned a corner that led to the chancellor's bedchamber. All was quiet. He listened but heard nothing. He turned to leave, then paused. The weak gleam of his lamp revealed something amiss.

The door to the chancellor's bedroom was slightly, so very slightly, open.

Only enough that the bolt wouldn't latch. Not enough to reveal anything going on inside. Which, from the sound of things, was nothing except snoring.

Surely it was nothing, the Imperial Butler thought. *A mistake anyone might make.*

But not anyone like the chancellor.

He was an old man, the chancellor, stooped, with a large belly and skinny limbs, cloudy eyes that peered through thick glasses, and a nose that dripped. After the former emperor had died young, the chancellor had practically raised his young son from boyhood while guarding the empire and its scepter of rule. If the emperor hadn't gone missing, he would've presented the scepter to him in just a few days' time.

If there was one thing the young butler knew about the chancellor, it was this: he was careful. Careful with the scepter, careful with papers, careful with secrets, careful with locks.

He would never go to sleep with his door ajar. Yet he must have, for still he snored like a drowsy bear.

The butler considered entering to check on him, but he hated to disturb or embarrass the old man over nothing. Surely everything was fine. Perhaps, as he aged, he was becoming forgetful. The butler reached for the doorknob to pull it gently shut.

Just before the bolt clicked, he heard it: a snort. A catch in the snore, then a muffling, then silence, as if a pillow had been thrown over the chancellor's head.

His fingers froze over the doorknob.

The bolt clicked. Too late to stop it.

The door wrenched open. Arms grabbed the butler and yanked him in.

His lamp slipped from his hand and snuffed out.

Something swiped his feet out from under him, and he toppled to the floor. The impact stunned him. He was young and no fighter, but he fought and kicked at the limbs of the assailants surrounding him. In the dark, there seemed to be a dozen. They kicked at him, then one huge person kneeled on his chest and belly, crushing his ribs till he could barely breathe.

He decided to stop resisting.

"It's that nosy kid butler," a voice said. "I *told* you he was spying on us."

Rudo, the butler thought, as the air in his lungs slowly left him.

"Did you get the signet ring?" another voice asked.

Baxa.

"Yanked it off the old man's finger myself," said the man squashing him.

Hacheming. His bullfrog voice couldn't be mistaken. Nor could the weight of his knees bearing down upon the butler's lungs.

"What about the scepter?" asked the first voice.

"Search for it, Rudo," was Baxa's reply. "Hacheming. Is that one knocked out?"

The butler went still as a corpse. Far better that these traitorous snakes should believe he was unconscious than use a poker from the fire to make sure of it.

The glow of a lamp shone pink through his eyelids now,

but the butler didn't peek. From the sounds they made, it was clear they were rifling through the room in search of the Imperial Scepter. What a calamity if they found it!

To think, he'd left Uncle Moon's farm to seek a more refined and elegant life for himself than keeping livestock. Pigs were genteel creatures compared with this.

He felt someone's breath on his face. They were examining him, the villains, as a wild dog might sniff its freshly killed prey.

"I think he's out," said Hacheming's voice, close by his ear.

"No sign of the scepter, though." Baxa cursed. "Grab them both by the ankles. There's a stairway at the end of the corridor. I'll keep watch until you're through the door. Then you can drag them both to the dungeons."

"Hey!" came Rudo's oily voice. "How do you get off so easy? Why do we have to do the hard part? Suppose they wake up and fight us?"

"Give them a thrashing if they do," Baxa purred. "But go easy on the older one. Until the scepter is found, we may need him. Then hurry back. With the chancellor's signet, it's time for us to start writing letters."

"Letters?" Hacheming huffed and wheezed as he dragged the old chancellor across his own bedroom floor. The butler felt his own ankles grabbed and tugged by hands that must have been Rudo's. He thought of the long, twisting stairs to the cellars, and then the dungeons below the cellars, with his head bumpety-bumping down the whole way, and nearly fainted.

"Starting," Baxa said, "with warnings about the dangerous criminal now roaming the countryside who kidnapped
the emperor. Short, but dangerous."

"Short and dangerous and stupid, you mean," rumbled
Hacheming.

Baxa chuckled. "If he's still alive, we'll smoke him out and
lock him away for good."

The other men laughed.

The emperor, the butler realized. *Our emperor.* They hadn't
killed him, but they were about to frame him as his own kidnapper and lock him in the dungeons from which no prisoner
had ever returned. The thought made the butler sick. True,
he may have been impossibly selfish and demanding, but he
was their emperor by rights. He'd inherited the throne. Not
Baxa. Not these ruthless traitors.

"Once we've locked him up," Baxa went on, "we'll make a
proclamation announcing the retirement of the old chancellor and naming me as the new one."

"Chancellor?" Rudo asked. "I thought you wanted to be
emperor."

Baxa sounded as smug as a cat that's given itself a nice
bath. "All things in time, my friends," he said. "Chancellor
today, emperor tomorrow. Soon, I'll be known throughout
the Three Continents as Baxa the Conqueror."

14

A STRANGE ROMANCE, AND A COW-COAXING COMPROMISE

BEGONIA WOKE SLOWLY. SHE'D BEEN DREAMING about the windmill in her village. A soft summer breeze fragrant with the smell of new hay and rose petals slowly turned the windmill's mighty blades. The breeze blew deliciously over her skin.

In warm, noisy puffs.

Of breath.

Cow breath.

She sat up in the early-morning light and collided with a moist cow snout.

"Phhht," said the snout in a welcoming sort of way.

"Alfalfa?" Begonia cried. "Is it really you?"

A large, long, loving lick from Alfalfa's enormous cow tongue was her reply. It felt like a kitty lick from Catnip, back home, times a hundred.

There was Alfalfa's huge cow head, white with a black spot on the forehead that looked to Begonia like a black splotch and nothing more.

Meanwhile, a tiny, flat, fuzzy head with huge eyes and blinky lashes poked around Alfalfa's head like a puppet on a long, bendy stick. Here, then there, left side, right side, up, down. Strange squawky sounds came from its throat. At the end of the long neck, Begonia saw the ostrich fluff his puffy brown feathers. Then she saw his powerful pink legs, almost taller than she was, and his terrifyingly huge, scaly, two-toed feet.

Begonia scrambled to her own five-toed feet and slowly backed away from the ostrich.

It returned to her then, the memory of last night, of clinging to her tree perch in terror, until this ostrich galloped in and saved them. He certainly wasn't Begonia's idea of a hero.

Was it only yesterday?

Alfalfa approached Begonia, lowing and mooing. Begonia noticed how full and heavy her milk-bag looked, and she forgot to be afraid of the ostrich.

"Key!" she cried. "Wake up! Breakfast is here!"

Key's shaggy head had accumulated a fresh crop of twigs, leaves, and mosses from his bed on the forest floor. He rose up, groggy and blinking, then saw Alfalfa.

"Hooray!" he cried. "I found your cow for you. I told you I would."

Begonia squatted beside her cow and began working the

udders gently. "What are you gibbering about? The cow found us. *You* didn't find anything."

"I dispute that point," said Key, "but we were talking of breakfast."

"Breakfast?" came the unpleasant voice of the short stranger. Him! That cowardly beast!

"Come on over here, Key," she called to him, "and I'll give you breakfast. Stick your head under Alfalfa's udder."

Key soon figured out what Begonia had in mind. He crawled underneath Alfalfa and lay there, face upward, mouth open.

Begonia aimed a shot of milk at his open mouth and squeezed.

"*Hffft!*"

"Oops," she said.

"That's my nose."

"Stop talking, and open wide," she ordered.

She milked and milked poor Alfalfa, who sighed with relief, while Key nearly drowned in his breakfast. The gray cat came over, sniffing, and mewed for its own meal. After a few missed shots, Begonia managed to squirt creamy milk straight into the kitty's mouth until it was satisfied. Then she squirted more at Key.

The ostrich bobbed his head down below Alfalfa for a better look at the milking operation. Begonia flinched as his huge googly eyes blinked at her.

The stranger sidled over, too—curious, yet keeping his

distance, with distaste curling his upper lip. Begonia stole a glance at him, her first full look at him in the light.

He was thin, and small of build. His pajamas had been purple, she decided, or possibly red, and the fabric was undoubtedly silk. It had once been shiny, but now the dirty, oily cloth stuck to his skinny frame. His hair clung to his head in greasy wisps, and two long, limp mustaches dripped from his upper lip like black rats' tails.

"Where did you buy that cat?" he demanded.

She laughed out loud. "Who buys a cat?" She aimed a long shot of milk at Key. "This cat chose me. She escaped from an imperial wagon full of terrified cats." She shook her head. "What kind of an emperor would be mean to cats?"

The stranger wrinkled his nose. "Cats are bad luck."

"Only to mice and rats," Begonia said. "Cats are the best luck a farm family could have."

"Pay attention, please," came Key's voice.

"Oh, did I squirt your eye?" asked Begonia. "Sorry."

Her own stomach began to grumble as the warm, creamy scent of milk filled her nose.

"Key, in your bag of stuff, you have a cup, haven't you? Fetch it here, and hold it for me so I can have some breakfast, too."

Key yielded his spot reluctantly to the cat and rummaged through his sack.

"Disgusting procedure," said the stranger. "Barbaric and revolting."

Squirt, squirt. The gray cat's tail flicked with pleasure.

"Don't you ever drink milk?" Begonia asked the stranger.

"When I wish to, but certainly not milk that comes from an animal!"

Begonia tried not to smile. "Where do you think *your* milk comes from, then?"

"From the finest porcelain pitchers," he said. "And they come from the kitchens."

Begonia hid her face against Alfalfa's warm flank so she wouldn't laugh. How could a full-grown person be so ignorant? Key returned with his tin cup and held it while Begonia filled it with milk. The joyful *ping, ping* of milk against metal made her mouth water.

She gulped down her warm milk and sighed with pleasure, filled another cup and drained it, too, then filled one for Key and another for herself, until they both felt satisfied. Begonia threw her arms around Alfalfa's neck and pressed her cheek against her warm hide.

"Here you are, old girl," she said. "What trouble you've given us!" She stroked her neck and back until her finger pricked something so sharp it made her cry out in pain. "Ow! Thorns!"

A nasty briar that Alfalfa had acquired on her journey grabbed hold of Begonia's finger and wouldn't let go. It took some fussing and a fair bit of bleeding before Begonia rescued herself and her cow from its vicious point.

"There you go, Alfalfa," she told the cow. "I'll wash all this blood off you at home." She ripped a strip from her faded pink scarf and wrapped it around her cut finger. Out of the corner of one eye, she saw the strange man pretend he wasn't watching her.

"Here, you," she called to him. "There's still plenty left. Since you don't have your kitchens or your pitchers today, wouldn't you like some of this milk? It's quite good, even if it does, er, come from a cow. You're hungry, aren't you?"

She filled a cup of foamy milk and held it out temptingly. He sniffed it like a twitchy rabbit, then seized the cup with both hands, guzzling the milk so desperately that half of it ran down his face. He cried out in dismay as milk dripped from the ends of his mustache.

Begonia laughed. "It's all right. There's plenty more." She filled him another cup, and another, and another. They passed the cup around once more, then lay there, each of them, with full bellies and fuzzy brains. The stranger moaned something about sugar buns and quail eggs.

Then they heard a faint sound of bells ringing through the trees.

Key looked up. "What's that?"

A faraway look of longing passed across the stranger's face. "It's the bell-ringing," he said, "for the celebration on the eve of the birthday of the . . . of the . . . the . . ."

"The emperor!" Begonia cried. "I forgot. We were all

going to go to the ceremonies in town today, after chores." She smiled sadly. "My little sister was so excited about her silly hair ribbons for the celebration."

"How old will the emperor be this year?" asked Key.

The stranger practically snarled at him. "You mean, you *don't know?*"

Key shrugged. "I've been wandering awhile. One loses track of less important things."

"Less *important!*" The stranger was incensed.

"He'll be twenty-two," Begonia explained. "That's why there's such a fuss. He'll receive the scepter of rule from the chancellor tomorrow."

The stranger sank to the ground and rested a forlorn chin on his knees.

"What's so special about twenty-two, anyway?" Key wondered aloud. "I've never understood it. I've got siblings and cousins that age and older, and I can tell you, I wouldn't trust them to run a family supper, much less an empire."

"If you'd ever learned your history, you'd know," said the stranger irritably.

"Pig farmers," said Key loftily, "don't see much reason to study history. At least, not the ones in my family."

"Some emperor from ages ago won a big battle at twenty-two, I think," Begonia said. "I can never remember which one. Too many of them have the same names. So confusing."

"Stupid peasants," muttered the stranger. "Well? Aren't you doing the worship ritual?"

They stared at him. "What, here?" asked Begonia. "Now?"

"At the chiming of the bells any time during the birthday week, all subjects must stop what they're doing, bow, and recite the Praise Hymn," the stranger said. "It's the law."

"*Subjects?*" Key repeated.

The stranger ignored him. "Bow."

Begonia felt ridiculous. But complying was easier than squabbling. They bowed.

"No, bow toward *me*," the stranger said.

What a pig! Begonia sighed. She might as well humor him. She bowed toward him.

He rubbed his hands together. "Good. Now, sing the song."

"How does the first line begin, again?" asked Begonia. "Something like *tah-tee-tah, tah-tee-tah, tum, tum, tum,* and then the cymbals . . ."

The stranger glowered at them, then cleared his throat and began to sing. "*O gracious, noble, kind and merciful* . . . Um . . ."

"*Emperor,*" supplied Key. "Obviously."

"*Your goodness blesses all our lives, O* . . ."

"*Emperor,*" Begonia said. "You keep forgetting the whole point of the line. Did you hit your head on something?"

"That's not how they describe him," said Key. "People say his parents were great rulers, but this one's a joke."

The stranger flushed red. "The Praise Hymn! *With the heart of a panther* . . ."

"Ugh," said Begonia. "Who wrote this nonsense?"

"And an arm of iron in battle, and the patience of a statue . . ."

"How is a statue patient?" asked Key. "Does it even have a choice?"

"Time for the chorus," the stranger said. "*We love thee, glorious . . .*" He glared at them. "Sing this part!"

Key and Begonia joined in. "*We love thee, glorious emperor!*"

But the stranger had faltered. He seemed to give up. Key tried to help. "It goes like this: *Em*-peror. You sing it like this: *Bum*-badum. *High*-and-low. Sing it after me. *Em*—"

"Oh, stop it!" the stranger cried. "Never mind!"

"If you say so," Begonia said. "It was your idea, you know."

The stranger gnashed his teeth. "Silence, little girl."

Begonia took a step back. "That's fine talk," she said, "for someone whose cow fed you."

"See here," said Key. "You can't speak so rudely to a damsel in distress! You'll only add to her distress."

"Oh, just stop it, Key," Begonia cried. "I can manage my own distress."

She turned away, for she couldn't bear the sight of either of them just then. It was time to go home. She would get Alfalfa and be off. But the sight of her cow made her stop and stare.

Alfalfa lay down in a mossy patch, and the ostrich sat with his huge body on the ground beside her, nuzzling his long neck around hers. *Snuggling*. Alfalfa made a loving little moo.

"Look at those two," Key said. "Like true lovers from a heroic ballad."

"It's the strangest thing I've ever seen," Begonia said.

"It's been like this since she first appeared yesterday," said the pajama man. "Absurd."

"Maybe," Begonia said slowly, "Alfalfa is confused and thinks your ostrich is her calf."

"But what does the ostrich think?" asked Key.

"In my experience," said Begonia, thinking of her chickens back home, "birds don't think much." She squared her shoulders. "Well, no matter. I have my Alfalfa now, so I'll take her home. You, Key, can be off to wherever you're going, and you, erm, sir, can travel on with your ostrich, without any further aggravation from my cow."

Key made a sound of protest, but Begonia marched over to where Alfalfa lay snuggled up with her ostrich friend.

"Come on, Alfalfa," Begonia called.

"Come on, girl! Let's go home!"

"Al-*fal*-fa!"

"Come on, Alfalfa, let's get moving."

"Alfalfa, you ox, get up!"

Key watched all this with a grin on his dirty face. "Are you sure she's really your cow?"

"Of course she's my cow!" Begonia addressed Alfalfa sternly. "Now you listen here, my girl. I've got aching feet, and a sore bottom, and a stiff neck, all because of you. So you are coming home with me *right now!*"

Begonia bellowed the last words into Alfalfa's face. Alfalfa chewed a bit of mossy grass as though she hadn't a care in the world. But the ostrich seemed upset by Begonia's outburst. He rose to his terrible feet, fluffed his wings angrily, and hissed at her.

An eight-foot-tall, two-toed, small-brained bird hissing its battle cry in your face is certainly an experience to remember. Not an experience to repeat. Begonia froze.

"Don't move," Key told her in a low voice.

"I'm *not* moving," she whispered. "Don't tell me what to do!"

The ostrich waved his wings a few times, just to show Begonia who was boss, then turned and wandered off as though nothing had happened. Alfalfa rose and ambled off after the ostrich.

Begonia shook her head in disgust. "She'll follow that stupid bird-monster, but not me, who's fed and milked her every morning of her life . . . Oh!" She snapped her fingers. "That's it!"

"That's what?" asked Key.

"That's how I'll get Alfalfa home," she said. "Alfalfa loves the ostrich. Goodness knows why. She follows him. Fine. I'll lead the ostrich to my house, and Alfalfa will follow."

She headed off after the odd pair of animal friends. The gray cat appeared from wherever it had been prowling and leaped up onto Begonia's shoulder.

The man in the pajamas scrambled to catch up with her. "See here," he said. "That's my ostrich. Not yours. You can't have him."

"I don't *want* your ostrich," Begonia said. "I just need to borrow him for a bit."

Key crashed through the underbrush after them. "Suppose the ostrich won't be easily led," he said. "Then you're right back to the same problem you had before."

Begonia turned to the stranger. "Can *you* lead the ostrich?"

The stranger shrugged. "He goes where I direct him," he said, "but I don't want to take him to your house. Why would I?"

She fumed silently. There had to be a way to borrow this ostrich long enough to get a homesick milkmaid and her love-struck cow back to Two Windmills. Poor Mumsy must be frantic by now, and oh, what Begonia wouldn't give for clean clothes and hot food and a washing-up!

Key tied the brass bell around Alfalfa's neck. Its chimes echoed mysteriously off tree trunks and reverberated through misty morning forest air. Up ahead, the ostrich moseyed forward with his funny, halting, waddling walk, pausing briefly to peck at a beetle here and nibble on fresh spring leaves there.

At least each step took her closer to the road home. They were headed farther along the same stream they'd followed yesterday. Soon they'd meet that other road, and if she turned, let's see, left, that would be east. No, northeast. Either way, it would take her back to the flowering bush where she first met Key, and from there she knew which road to take home.

She turned toward the stranger. "Where are you headed, anyway?"

He scowled. "My destination is none of your business."

"I only wondered," she said slowly, "if it's near where I'm bound. There's safety in numbers. Let the panthers eat us instead of you, right? If you came to my home, if the panthers hadn't eaten me, Mumsy—my mother—would feed you a hot meal and wash your clothes."

Key's drooping spine turned to water at this idea. "She would?" he sighed. "Would she feed *me* a hot meal and wash *my* clothes, too?"

Begonia groaned.

"Look, sir," Key said to the stranger. "We can't very well not call you anything. It feels impolite, and a romantic is always polite, come what may. Courteous to the death! That's what we are. So give us something we can call you."

The man's lips twitched, as though he were at war with them. He grew so exasperated that he tugged at his hair with both hands. Then he lifted his head, as though he'd had a new idea.

"Lumi," he said slowly, as if testing the sound. "*Lumi!* Yes, Lumi. If you must call me something, you may call me Lumi."

The gray cat on Begonia's shoulder yowled.

"The kitty doesn't like your name," Begonia observed. "She needs a name, too. Mumsy would name her after some plant or other. So I'll call her Stormcloud." She grinned.

"I've never gotten to name anything before." The kitty chewed Begonia's hair in reply. "I think she likes it."

"Stormcloud has a name, and now, Lumi," said Key, "you have one, too. Excellent. Now tell us a little bit about yourself. Where you're from, where you're going. What your story is."

"Why should I?" demanded Lumi, if that were really his name, which Begonia doubted.

"I gave you breakfast," she reminded him.

"Hah," said the little man. "Do you know how many people usually bring me breakfast?"

"Six," said Key.

Begonia giggled, but their companion looked surprised. "Yes," he said. "You guessed it."

They waited. They heard no other sound but the chirping of morning birds and the crunching of claws, hooves, and feet through last autumn's fallen leaves.

"Tell us where home is, Lumi," Begonia begged.

"I was rudely driven from my . . . home," he said at last. "I was violently robbed of my . . . home." He took a deep breath. "I am trying to get back to my . . . home."

Begonia and Key exchanged puzzled glances. Key whispered, "He forgets words a lot."

"Well," Begonia said slowly, "that's sad. I'm very sorry to hear it. Did you ever ask any people you met along the way for help?"

He scowled. "I tried, many times. In Mackerel City, I was

forced to ask low persons for sustenance. Fishwives and bakers and such. But they were disgustingly rude. When I couldn't . . . when they didn't understand my answers to their questions, the stupid peasants, they threw things at me and drove me out of the city. They called me a thief for helping myself to food, when it's mine by rights!"

Key's eyebrows rose. "You mean, you stole loaves of bread and so forth, and they got mad at you for it?"

"Can you believe it?" demanded Lumi. "They threatened to have soldiers arrest me! I only just managed to get away. I avoid people now."

Key gestured to himself and Begonia. "We're people."

"No, you're not."

Up ahead, Alfalfa's white tail swished from side to side, and her swaying rump did the same while her bell tinkled. Beyond her, the ostrich's big brown body bobbed along atop his impossible legs. His head and neck hung low as he pecked for breakfast, so he looked like a headless body hovering on stilts, as though he'd lost his head completely.

Begonia began to fear she'd lost hers.

But at least they were moving. Now, if she could just move them toward home.

She stuck her hands into her pockets and felt the parchment curl of the mapmaker's gift.

The mapmaker. Now there was an idea.

"Lumi," she said, "it sounds like what you need is a good map of the empire, if you're going to find your home."

Lumi gestured to the mapless forest all around them. "Where do you suggest I find one?"

"In my village of Two Windmills," she said, "which we could reach by suppertime, there lives a master mapmaker. He has piles and piles of maps. Here's one he gave me." She offered him her own small map.

"If you described your home to him, Master Mapmaker could show you the way and give you a map to get there." She watched his face closely to see if she was getting anywhere. "Of course, before you visited the mapmaker, you'd probably want a bath, and warm towels, and clean clothes, and some home-cooked supper, which Mumsy will be only too happy to give you."

Once again, Key moaned with anticipation. "It sounds like heaven. I can't wait. Are there meatballs? I long for meatballs!"

Begonia ignored him. "Just a day's walk, and we're there."

Up ahead, the trees were thinning. More morning light filtered through. They were reaching the end of the woods, which meant soon they'd reach the road, and perhaps Lumi would take his ostrich another way, with Alfalfa following them in all likelihood. It was now or never.

"You'll *love* our village," she said, doubting he could actually love anything.

"Hmm," said Lumi. "Two Windmills, you say? I've never heard of it."

"We're a friendly village," Begonia said. "Very peaceful."

Lumi's stomach let out a loud rumble. He plucked at his grimy clothes, then fingered one limp mustache. He drew himself up tall.

"I shall accompany you to this Two Windmills of yours," said he. "No doubt it's a backward place, or I would know of it. But I shall visit, inspect it, and demand of its occupants a bath, and clothes, and a map. I have made up my mind."

15

AN ANXIOUS TRAVELER,
AND HER HURRIED JOURNEY

LONG BEFORE THE SUN ROSE IN THE EASTERN sky and cast its rosy glow over Peony's round cheeks as she slept like an angel beside her, Chrysanthemumsy had made her decision.

She would go look for Begonia.

She hadn't slept all night for fretting about her daughter. Any pale comfort she'd taken from Madame Mustard-maker's words the night before had faded long before the moon reached the peak of its sweep across the sky.

She should've gone sooner. She shouldn't have listened to Madame Mustard-maker. The whole thing was highly suspicious. She should've gone searching last night. Who could tell what terrors might befall a young girl alone in the world in the dark of night? But Chrysanthemumsy knew she couldn't have found her at night. If only she had eyes to see in the dark like Catnip.

If only she had never sent Begonia in the first place. True, Begonia had successfully brought Alfalfa home in the past, but any mother should have realized that finding a wandering cow could turn into a wild-goose chase.

It was just that Begonia was so reliable, so capable. It was easy to entrust her with tasks and responsibilities. Usually, she accomplished them all without a hitch.

Chrysanthemumsy moved softly from the bed, so as not to disturb little Peony, and went outside. She asked Grand-mother Flummox to come sit with Peony and take care of the milking and eggs in her absence. The neighbor, though still mending from her cold, came immediately. All of Two Windmills knew by now that Begonia hadn't come home, and they prayed that the ancestor spirits would watch over her and bring her safely back.

Chrysanthemumsy packed some food and a bottle of water in a sack, threw it over her shoulder, and headed toward the village. Begonia had gone that way, she knew, and passed straight through town. Witnesses had been able to tell her that much yesterday.

She walked all morning, until the sun had nearly reached its peak and her feet felt heavy with fatigue. Poor Begonia! To have faced so long a journey alone, and so young!

I'm coming, daughter. Over and over, she willed the words to travel from her heart to Begonia's, to give her comfort and strength. May the words find her safe. May her feet follow soon after.

16

MORE BICKERING, AND A BIRD-BACK BOOST

BEGONIA, LUMI, KEY, AND THE ANIMALS stumbled through the thinning trees and found themselves facing the road. The ostrich blinked at the bright midday sunlight, while Alfalfa got to work munching succulent grass and clover growing along the road's margins.

"Help me up," ordered Lumi.

"Up where?" asked Key.

"Onto my ostrich, you dunce," was Lumi's reply. "Did you really think I would walk *on foot* all day long?"

Begonia looked to her left down the long corridor of road that snaked through the trees. She consulted her map. Yes, left was the way to go. This path would lead eventually to the fork in the road and the purple bush, through small villages, and then to her home, her barn, her bedroom. Mumsy could sort out the twin nuisances of Lumi and Key, and life would go back to normal.

Key, however, was engaged in conversation with Lumi.

"Really?" he said. "You *ride* that ostrich? It actually lets you ride it?"

Lumi's nose poked the clouds. "Of course it does. It's my ostrich."

Key was fascinated. "Have you always ridden ostriches? Since you were little?" His eyes lit up. "Say, is that what you do for a living? Ride ostriches in races? You're just the build for the job."

"Enough of your prattle. Help me *up*, I say!" demanded Lumi. "What is the matter with you two? I never knew peasants could be so stupid and unhelpful."

Something inside Begonia made a quiet little explosion. She couldn't say why. Perhaps it was walking all morning after nothing but milk for breakfast. Perhaps it was sleeping on the damp forest floor after nearly becoming a panther's midnight meal. Begonia had had enough. Lumi had certainly said worse. But this was one remark too many. She was done with trying to placate this tyrant.

"What's the matter with *you*, that you treat people so rudely?" she said. "You act like you're the emperor himself, bossing and complaining so much. But I'm sure the emperor at least knows better than to act like such a spoiled baby, or no one would ever follow a word he says."

Lumi's lips quivered, which made his mustaches wiggle.

The effect was not unlike the sniffing, twitchy snout of a whiskered rat. Stormcloud, who evidently disapproved of rising voices, leaped from Begonia's shoulder to the ground.

"Nobody talks that way to me," he said. "I shan't help you if you talk that way to me. You can figure out how to get your useless cow home without my ostrich."

"Then we won't help you get up onto his back," replied Begonia. "And you can just go back to wandering in circles and sleeping hungry under the stars, with panthers for company, while you try to find your home."

"Um, Begonia?"

"Not now, Key!" she cried. "And furthermore, I'm beginning to have some sympathy for whoever it was that drove you out of your home. Who can blame them, if they had to live with you? You're the most selfish person I ever met."

Key hopped from left foot to right. "Begonia—"

"What do you know about anything, you silly little girl?" Lumi's face bunched up like a prune, and he stuck his tongue out at Begonia. "Great men like me don't listen to the prattle of brainless little maidens. Great men like me don't even allow little girls into their presence because they're completely useless."

Key tugged on her sleeve. "Begonia . . ."

She whirled on him and unleashed all the anger that she would've liked to blast at Lumi. "*What*, Key? What's so important that you have to tell me *right now?*"

He pointed down the road. "The animals are gone."

They all turned. Sure enough, there was no sign of the ostrich or the cow.

"Which way did they go?" cried Lumi. "Why weren't you watching?"

"I was watching," said Key indignantly. "I tried to tell you. They went that way."

Lumi and Begonia bolted down the road toward the left, with Key following along after them. Lumi's sprint didn't last long. Begonia, however, ran well and kept going until she came around a bend and nearly collided with Alfalfa. The ostrich, who had one wing thrown over the cow, for all the world like a young man with his arm around a sweetheart, ballooned out his throat and made a low hooting sound at Begonia. Then he turned around, spread his wings wide, and ran straight for her. On powerful, panther-kicking legs.

She backed away, then turned and ran. She was no match for his speed. The ostrich loped easily behind her, waving his menacing wings as a warning, until a lowing moo from Alfalfa halted him, and he turned and trotted back to his cow.

Begonia wiped her forehead with her apron.

She caught her breath and waited to make sure the ostrich wouldn't change his mind. "I found them," she shouted.

Key jogged into view, followed eventually by a red-faced Lumi, and finally by Stormcloud.

"It's not that I don't agree with you completely," Key said as they watched the huffing man approach, "about Lumi being an absolute terror, but I think we should probably stop fighting with him—and by 'we' I mean 'you,' but a romantic doesn't like to criticize a damsel, not directly. Let's just get him up on his ostrich."

Begonia rolled her eyes and thought up a juicy retort for Key. Then she sighed. "What if we get him up on his ostrich, and they just run off and abandon us?"

Key shrugged. "At least we'll be rid of him."

Begonia grinned. "You make an excellent point."

"Maybe with the ostrich gone, Alfalfa will follow you home," added Key. "But I doubt the ostrich will leave his lady friend. Personally, I wouldn't." He glanced sidelong at Begonia. "If I were an ostrich, that is."

Lumi reached them just then. Begonia swallowed the things she would have liked to say to him. "If you stand on that fallen log near the woods," she told him, "we can help boost you onto the ostrich's back."

To her surprise, he nodded and went straight to the tree. He clambered clumsily atop the large fallen trunk and whistled to the ostrich. He came. Key and Begonia hurried to help, and together they boosted and hoisted Lumi's legs up over the bird's body and under his wings. The ostrich didn't like the whole affair, and neither did Begonia, for Lumi badly needed a bath. But, finally, they got him mounted, and Lumi nudged him onward down the road. The ostrich complied but swiveled his head around to make sure Alfalfa was following.

This was the scene: An eight-foot tall bird, picking his way along the dusty highway, with an alarmingly mustached rider in filthy red silk pajamas bobbing along atop his fluffy back. Behind them, a white cow with a black spot following close by, tinkling the bell on her neck and mooing the moos of cow romance. Behind her, a rather dirty milkmaid in a dress that had probably once been blue, and an apron that would never again be white, trailing a pink scarf from her long dark hair, which was batted at occasionally by the gray cat that seemed permanently affixed to her shoulder. Behind girl and cat, a tall, slouching boy, with a sack over his shoulder and his hair so full of twigs and leaves he looked more like a shambling sapling than a human being.

This is what anyone watching them would have seen.

As they came around the next bend in the road, this is what someone else did see.

"Well, I never," said a booming voice as an elegantly dressed rider came into view and pulled up the reins of his glossy black horse. "Never in all my days did I see a party like this traveling along the emperor's highways. And I've seen some extraordinary sights. You can be sure of that. I'm Poka, proprietor of Poka's Carnival of Curiosities, at your service. Pleased to meet you."

17

ANOTHER STRANGE ROMANCE, AND ITS TRAGIC INTERRUPTION

CHRYSANTHEMUMSY WALKED AS QUICKLY AS she could, but even her urgency to find her daughter didn't stop her from growing weary. Somewhere past the hamlet of Mossy Well, she came to a shady spot under a grove of trees and sat down on a boulder to drink some water and catch her breath before continuing. She was aware, dimly, that this was a lovely spot, with green grasses dancing in the breeze, birds singing through the trees, and the carved roof of an open-air temple peeking up just beyond a rise in the ground. But she had no stomach for sightseeing today.

Resting her feet awakened her anxious heart. Would she find Begonia? Would she be all right? A tear dropped from her chin and sank into the dust of the road. She heard footsteps approaching from the other direction. She quickly wiped her face and rubbed her eyes.

It was a wedding procession, bound for the temple. A bride in a colorful robe walked alongside a tall groom in a white tunic. A priest and a priestess accompanied them, but no other guests or relatives, which was strange. The bride carried a fresh orchid in one hand and held a baby clamped to her hip with the other.

Any other day, the sight would have made Chrysanthemumsy smile. Today, she was glad that bowing low would hide her face.

"Blessings on you, on your families, and on the family that is born today," she told the couple when they paused to look at her.

The bride took a long look at Chrysanthemumsy.

"You look sad," she proclaimed. "Today is no day for sadness. Here. Hold my baby."

And without waiting for Chrysanthemumsy to respond or protest, she deposited the child in her lap.

Rare is the woman who has rocked her own babies to sleep who can refuse any baby thrust into her arms. The hands and heart reach out before the brain has time to wonder if this is a convenient moment. The wise, dark eyes and smiling face of this child warmed Chrysanthemumsy's heart. But she couldn't allow any pause in her hunt for Begonia.

"Ma'am," she said, hurrying after the couple, which was heading over the grassy knoll to the temple, "any other day I'd be most glad to tend your baby, truly. But my daughter is missing, and I have to go find her."

The bride gazed at her thoughtfully. "Was your daughter walking in search of a missing white cow?"

Chrysanthemumsy hugged the baby tightly to her. "How did you know?"

"If it weren't for her, I wouldn't have met my future husband," the bride said. She took her groom by the hand. "He's a woodcutter, and he likes babies. Isn't he handsome? Say hello, dear."

The woodcutter mopped his forehead with his sleeve. "Hello."

Chrysanthemumsy's head began to spin. "My daughter . . . introduced you to your . . . to him?"

The woman nodded. "Just yesterday."

"Just *yesterday*?"

The couple blushed at each other.

"You're joking," Chrysanthemumsy said.

The woman didn't take her eyes off her beau. "Not joking."

"Oh." Chrysanthemumsy was at a loss. "Well, then, congratulations."

The priestess cleared her throat. "It is time to begin."

"But when yesterday? Where? Was she all right? Can you point me toward the spot?"

The bride took her place beside her woodcutter groom and took his arm, then turned and gave a disapproving "Shh" to Chrysanthemumsy.

Chrysanthemumsy was stuck. She couldn't set the baby down and leave. She had to know whatever this strange person could tell her about her daughter's whereabouts. And she couldn't very well interrupt a wedding for it. So she took her place toward the rear of the temple and bounced the baby up and down to make him smile. A smiling baby can gladden any heart, and she needed all the hope she could find.

She stood behind a marble pillar and whispered to the child.

"If only you could talk, little man," she said. "Did you meet my Begonia? Did you?"

The baby beamed and giggled.

"So you're getting a new papa today, aren't you?" she whispered. "Do you like him?"

Again, the baby beamed.

"That's good. It's plain to see your mama likes him." She smiled, not unaware that she was carrying on a conversation with an infant. "He's so smitten with her, he can't get a word out. Some men are like that around ladies. But you won't be, will you, my fine little fellow?" As if in reply, the baby babbled happily.

She tuned an ear toward the words of the priestess and the priest. The ceremony was nearly at an end. The priest sang the short song of love sung at every wedding. The newly married couple took each other by the hand, and then they were told to kiss. The woodcutter had to bow quite low to reach his new bride's lips. His cheeks flushed red. But both of them looked so happy to be married that Chrysanthemumsy couldn't help but smile.

"What's going on here?" demanded a loud voice.

Chrysanthemumsy slipped behind her pillar and held the baby close. Imperial soldiers! Four of them, marching into the temple. The echoes of their stamping boots shattered the peace that ought to fill a temple always. Soldiers at a wedding? It was unheard of!

"A wedding, good sirs," said the priestess, "as you can see."

"Did you file the proper marriage paperwork?" demanded the leader. "Did you pay the wedding tax?"

The new couple and the priest and priestess gazed at one another in bewilderment.

"Paperwork?" asked the priest.

"What tax?" demanded the bride.

"Twenty silver buckles, to be paid by the groom, for the privilege of marrying one of the emperor's female subjects."

"What?" roared the woodcutter, bashful no longer.

The soldier read from a scroll. The broken wax seal on it still seemed new and fresh.

"Twenty silver buckles, to be paid by the wife, each time

she bears a child," he continued, "for the privilege of adding a new subject to the emperor's realm."

"Doesn't the emperor want new subjects?" asked the new wife.

The soldier grinned. "Of course he does," he said. "Lots of them."

Chrysanthemumsy shook her head. Such taxes were unheard of! The baby in her arms, as if sensing her disgust, began to make fussing sounds. Chrysanthemumsy hushed him the best she could. Suppose they demanded a tax for babies already born?

"Since when?" demanded the woodcutter, and there was no mistaking the challenge in his voice. He was a tall and brawny man, who could no doubt do great damage with his ax, but his ax wasn't here. And these four soldiers were fully armed.

"Since the new chancellor came into power," answered the soldier.

"What new chancellor?" demanded the woodcutter. "Whoever he is, his taxes and fines'll ruin the empire!"

"We army men like him just fine," the soldier answered. "He's doubled the pay of every soldier in the empire. Now, are you going to pay your marriage tax, or aren't you? The fine doubles if you pay it after the marriage." His smile wasn't pleasant at all. "But I'll cut you a break, since the rule is so new. Thirty silver buckles, and we'll call it even."

"But we didn't know," protested the woodcutter's new wife.

"Ignorance is no excuse," said the soldier.

The woodcutter clenched his fists. "Did you just call my wife ignorant?"

"No fighting in the sacred temple!" cried the priestess. "You'll offend the ancestors!"

The soldiers' hands went to the pommels of their clubs.

"Out! Out!" the priestess shrieked.

The party stumbled out of the cool reverence of the temple and into glaring sunlight. Chrysanthemumsy stayed inside the temple's shadows with the baby, peering around the doorway to watch.

"Now," said the soldier, "are you going to pay? Or do we need to take you for a ride?"

The breath in the woodcutter's nostrils reminded Chrysanthemumsy of a snorting bull.

"I can't pay," he said. "But even if I could pay, I wouldn't."

His new bride covered her face with her hands.

"Take him in, men," ordered the soldier. "Some time in the Imperial Dungeons ought to cool him off."

The woodcutter fought bravely and gave more than one soldier a punch in the jaw that would loosen teeth, and jabs in the eyes that would surely leave bruises for days. But in the end, he was no match for their weapons, and he was too young and full of life to seriously want to die. They tied his wrists behind his back and prodded him toward the road. His head hung low, and he turned to gaze sorrowfully at his new wife, still clutching her drooping orchid.

The captors and their prize vanished over the hillock. Chrysanthemumsy ventured out of the temple and placed an arm around the abandoned bride's shoulders.

"I'm so sorry," she said softly.

The woman wiped her eyes with a square of cloth.

"Another short marriage." She sighed. "It seems to be my lot in life." She reached for her baby, who went joyfully into her arms. Poor mite. He knew nothing of what had just gone on.

"Well," she continued, "it is what it is. And there go my plans for the day. I was going to make my new husband a dinner of chicken noodle soup. But there's little point in that now, is there?"

Chrysanthemumsy shook her head. "Don't you want to try to get your husband out of prison?"

"Does anyone ever leave the dungeons?" she answered sadly. "Of course I want to get him out, but I haven't so much as a half-buckle."

Chrysanthemumsy had only just met this woman, but after witnessing this scene, she felt sisterly toward her.

"It's an awful feeling, being powerless to help the ones we love," she said. Thoughts of Begonia swam into her mind, and her eyes filled suddenly with tears.

The woman gazed into Chrysanthemumsy's grief. "You're afraid for your daughter," she remembered aloud. Then she straightened up. "Our paths lie in the same direction. Lotus City is this way, and so's your girl. I might as well help you find her. Come on. Let's go. Here. You hold the baby."

18

A CARNIVAL MAN,
AND A TREACHEROUS PLAN

OKA, PROPRIETOR OF POKA'S CARNIVAL OF Curiosities, swung one shiny-booted leg over his horse's back and jumped to the ground.

He was stout, though strong, with a broad, shiny face and a smile filled with teeth. He wore a purple striped vest over his impressive trunk, with a vivid blue coat and tails and tie, and bright red trousers. He lifted his tall hat to the newcomers, then rubbed his hands together. Keeping his horse on a lead, he approached Begonia's party.

"I know what that is," he said, pointing. "That's a postrich. What a beauty! Seen pictures of 'em in books, but never in Camellion. Temple bells, but he's big. Lookit those legs! They say"—he leaned in close—"they say the emperor has a few in his private menagerie. What I wouldn't give to get a peek at that. And sell tickets to it. Har! Har!"

"It's not a postrich. It's an ostrich," said Begonia.

He patted her head as though she were a poodle. "You're dealing with Poka, an expert in animals, rare and strange. If I say it's a postrich, it's a postrich."

Stormcloud hissed at Poka. Begonia secretly agreed with her.

Poka surveyed the entire group. "There's a story here. I'm sure of it," said he. "What would cause a postrich to allow a rider? Why is this cow following the bird? And why are these poor little orphans tagging along?"

Begonia said nothing. Poka didn't deserve an answer. For once, Key kept silent also. Lumi urged his ostrich forward, and their party kept on going. But Poka would not be so easily deterred. He and his horse walked along beside them.

"You, sir," he said, addressing Lumi, "appear to be the man in charge. Who might you be? And tell me, how much for that postrich?" He reached his hand into his blue coat and pulled out a small pouch of black velvet. "I'll give you fifteen silver buckles for him." Inside, Begonia could hear the heavy chink of buckles, a sound she hadn't had much occasion to hear before. She'd only heard the clink of little copper buttons, and rarely that.

Lumi pointed his nose in the air and kept going. For once, Begonia blessed his arrogance.

"Family pet, I take it," said Poka, trotting along beside them. "Sentimental value. All right, then." He pulled another, fatter purse from a deeper pocket. "Twenty buckles? Name your price."

"You're wasting your breath," Begonia told him. "He doesn't like people."

"But everybody likes me," protested Poka. "I'm the man who's made a million smiles!"

Poka planted himself directly in the ostrich's path. Stupid of him, Begonia thought. His face now was red and sweating, but he kept his teeth beaming full-force at Lumi.

"I tell you, sir, it's downright selfish of you to hog a fine specimen such as that all to yourself," said Poka, "when he could be the prize display at Poka's Carnival of Curiosities, bringing pleasure and delight to one and all throughout the empire, old and young and young at heart. In Poka's carnival, he'd be treated better than the emperor. He'd be the belle of the ball, the star of the show, the plum in a plum cake like Mother used to bake. 'Poka's Prize Postrich,' we'd call him, and I'd have the sign painted in big orange letters, with black trim. Now, let's make a deal. Twenty-five silver buckles? What do you say?"

When Lumi made no response, Poka glanced back toward the rest of the company.

"I tell you what. I'll even throw in extra for the cow and the two urchins. Take them right off your hands, and you'll walk away a carefree man with *thirty* silver buckles jingling in your pocket. Thirty silver buckles, and that's my final offer."

"We're not for sale!" Begonia cried. "Why don't you leave us alone?"

"A feisty one!" cried Poka. "I'll find a good use for her. She can sell tickets at the carnival and make sure nobody tries to sneak in without paying."

Lumi's disdain for Poka overcame his snobbish silence at last. "Make way, you . . . you *tradesman*," he said with a sneer. "Begone."

Begonia almost cheered for Lumi. That proved what kind of a day she was having.

"I don't think you even have a carnival," she said. "Where is it?"

"Coming along behind me, maybe half a mile back," said Poka. "It's a slow operation, toting all those smelephants and frynoceroses. But with Poka's Carnival of Curiosities, every exhibit, from the man-eating tigers to the dancing bearded lady, travels in elegant style."

"Step aside, vulgar entertainer, and let us pass," ordered Lumi. "Our journey won't keep for someone such as yourself."

Poka's toothy smile faltered, and a hard gleam flickered across his eyes. He pocketed his money pouches. "As you wish, as you like," he said, and rubbed his hands together once more. "Poka lives only to please."

Just then, the ostrich's head popped up and strained forward. Alfalfa sniffed the wind.

At first, Begonia could make out no sign of what the

animals had noticed. Then she caught the sound of faraway hoofbeats, growing louder every second.

"That carnival of yours travels fast," said Key.

Poka examined the ostrich from every side. He pulled a short ruler from his pocket and took a rough measurement of the bird's legs. "That's not my carnival," he said. "Only soldiers ride that fast."

Lumi stiffened. A cloud of fear crossed his face. He nudged the ostrich off the road and straight into the woods. Alfalfa followed, and Begonia and Key brought up the rear, but they lingered, crouching in the underbrush to see who was coming in such a rush.

"What's the hurry, friends?" Poka called after them.

The hoofbeats grew louder, cantering at a rapid clip. Four horses came into view. Their riders slowed to a stop at the sight of Poka standing by the edge of the road, holding his horse's rein. The riders wore black helmets and red tunics, with the clubs and short swords of imperial soldiers belted to their sides.

"Good morning, good sirs," Poka called to them.

"Are you with that traveling circus we just passed?" asked one of the soldiers.

Poka bowed. "Indeed, I am; Poka's my name, proprietor of Poka's Carnival of—"

"We're searching for a runaway," the soldier barked. "A villain who kidnapped the emperor."

Begonia's breath caught in her throat. A violent kidnapper,

roaming around these highways? One who had kidnapped the *emperor*?

"No!" Poka removed his hat and placed it over his heart. "So close to his grand birthday? How dreadful!"

Another soldier produced a roll of paper. "We just received word from the palace. There's a description of him here. Let's see." The soldier, who didn't seem to be the sharpest reader, scanned the paper with a thick finger. "'Short, puny man.'"

From their hiding place in the bushes, Key sniggered. "Sounds like Lumi."

"Shh."

The soldier kept reading. "Where is it, let's see. Ah. 'Nasty temper.'"

Key elbowed Begonia. "Quite the coincidence, eh?"

"Be *quiet!*"

"'Narrow face,'" the reader went on. "'Long mustaches.'"

Key bit his hand to squelch his laughing. "Too funny!" he wheezed. "Sounds like we're traveling with a kidnapper and his ostrich, eh?"

Begonia glared at him.

"A kidnapper and his ostrich," he repeated. His eyebrows rose, and his eyeballs looked ready to pop. "A *kidnapper* and his ostrich? A 'short, ugly, nasty-tempered man—' You don't suppose . . . ?"

Begonia clamped her hand over Key's mouth before he could say more.

"Quiet down and settle down," she ordered. "A dangerous kidnapper? Please! He's nothing but a big baby!"

"Yes, but . . ."

Begonia watched Poka stroke his chin. "Lots of people are short, with mustaches," she said.

"And nasty tempers?"

"Maybe they go with the mustaches."

Across the way, Poka placed his hat back on his head. "Gentlemen," he told the soldiers, "I'm so glad you're here. Why, to think that I just came within an inch of my life! It just goes to show you can't ever trust anybody. The very man you're looking for just kidnapped a priceless postrich from my carnival. Held me at knifepoint! I fought him off, but he was vicious. My animals mean the world to me, so I followed him here on horseback. Those postriches can travel powerful fast, though. The kidnapper just escaped into these woods."

He pointed straight at where Begonia and Key crouched in the bushes.

"Why, that lying sneak!" Begonia hissed.

"Thank you," cried the soldiers. "We'll catch him now!"

"But don't harm my postrich, whatever you do!" cried Poka.

The soldiers spurred their horses toward the woods. "What's a postrich, anyway?" one of them called out.

"You'll know it when you see it," Poka called after them. "I'm counting on you, gentlemen, in consideration of my valuable help, to bring me back my giant bird."

The mounted soldiers entered the forest.

Begonia and Key made themselves as small as possible and held their breath.

The soldiers paused to consider which way to go.

"Look at those footprints," one called to the leader.

"A cow made those, I'd say," said his companion.

The first shook his head. "No, *those*."

Another soldier whistled in amazement. " 'Giant bird,' he said? What kind of a monster is this?"

"The bird can't be as dangerous as someone who could fight his way past the palace guards and kidnap the emperor," the leader said. "Follow that trail." Moments later, they were gone.

19

ONE BAD BUSINESS,
AND THEN ANOTHER

"POOR ALFALFA," BEGONIA MOANED. "WHAT will they do to her?"

"Leave her alone, I imagine," said Key. "It's Lumi and the postrich, I mean, ostrich, that are in danger. But perhaps *they're* in danger if Lumi is the kidnapper . . ."

"Would you stop that? He couldn't kidnap a cockroach crawling underneath his shoe."

"Don't look down on cockroaches," said Key. "I've been living on them for a while now. They have a pleasing crunch, though I'd choose meatballs any day, given the option. But my point is this: those soldiers will *think* he's the kidnapper; and if they catch him, he'll rot out the rest of his days in the emperor's dungeons."

Begonia tried to think. Didn't a rat fink like Lumi deserve

a spell in the dungeons? A week or two there might do him a world of good.

But if the dungeon rumors were true, he'd be there a lifetime longer than a week or two.

"If the soldiers take Lumi away and give the ostrich to Poka," she thought aloud, "then I'll be able to take Alfalfa home and be done with all this nonsense."

Key watched her with a curious expression. It annoyed her. But the more she tried to ignore him, the more piercingly he stared.

The torment was killing her. "What?" she demanded.

Key spoke slowly. "*Are you sure* you don't think Lumi could be a kidnapper?"

"Positive."

His searching gaze made Begonia squirm. "Really, really sure?"

She folded her arms across her chest. "So sure I'd bet my best laying hen on it."

He shook his head sadly. "Then how, you'll forgive me for asking, for a romantic never wants to distress a damsel already in distress, but how, I say, can you stand by and do nothing?"

She couldn't answer.

And she wouldn't look him in the eye.

"Did you really live on cockroaches?" she asked. "That's disgusting."

"Don't change the subject."

Down the road, they heard the creaks and rattles of a caravan of wagons. Animal noises filled the air. Something roared, and something else trumpeted a high squeal.

"The carnival," she said. "That stinker Poka! Using the emperor's soldiers to help him steal Lumi's ostrich. He's got a lot of nerve." She sighed. It irked her to no end to concede that Key was right. "All right then, Mr. Conscience, let's go help Lumi, if we're not too late."

They took off, crashing through the brush, racing through the woods. Begonia doubted they could catch up to the soldiers' horses, but they soon heard men's voices close at hand.

"Um, Begonia," Key called to her. "What exactly is our plan?"

She leaped over a fallen tree limb and kept on running. "How should I know?"

They burst upon Lumi, the ostrich, and Alfalfa, surrounded by soldiers, who seemed astonished at the sight of the young people. Alfalfa mooed, the ostrich hooted, and Lumi hurled orders and insults at the men, but they only tightened their perimeter around him and reached for coils of rope tied to their saddles.

". . . because I could swear I've seen your face somewhere before," a soldier was saying as he skewered Lumi with a piercing look. "Only, I look again and I'm not so sure."

"Probably been in trouble with the law before," the captain said. "Scumbag like you."

Lumi's face was so dirty, Begonia thought, not even his mirror would recognize him.

Begonia seized an opening in the conversation. "Uncle Lumi! Uncle Lumi!" she squealed. "I've been trying all morning to find you, *Uncle* Lumi!" She ran to him through the ring of soldiers and hugged his ankle. It was the only part of him that she could reach, perched as he was on the ostrich.

She looked at the soldiers. "I'm Begonia, and this is my, er, cousin, Key. That's my cow, Alfalfa. But what do you men want with my Uncle Lumi?"

She realized she'd never spoken so many words at once to a group of adults in her life. And soldiers, at that. Alone in the woods, confronting half the emperor's army!

Not quite half. But still.

"Back away, little girl," said the one in charge. "We're taking this man into custody."

She gulped down her jitters. "But why?"

The leader dismounted and loosened his rope. "For kidnapping the emperor."

Begonia gasped. "The emperor, *kidnapped*? On the eve of his birthday? How awful!"

"It's true," said the captain. He pointed to Lumi. "And that's the fiend who did it. We've got witnesses to prove it. Trusted palace officials."

"What do you mean," cried Lumi, sputtering with rage, " 'kidnapping the . . . the . . .' "

"Emperor," snapped the captain. "You heard me."

Lumi laughed bitterly. "Absurd!"

"Yes, absurd," Begonia said. "Uncle Lumi couldn't kidnap a duck."

"I could, too," said Lumi.

"But if he kidnapped the emperor, where's the emperor?" Begonia pressed her questions, one by one. "Why aren't they both in hiding somewhere?"

The captain shrugged. "Look, we have our orders. We don't have to justify them to you."

Begonia tried to think. She lacked practice in lying. "Our Uncle Lumi traveled with us all day yesterday from the village of Two Windmills. We certainly never saw the emperor. I'm on an errand to sell this cow, and he . . ." She racked her brain. "He is training his new ostrich."

"Postrich," corrected one of the soldiers. "And we know he kidnapped that bird, too. Don't think you can fool us."

Lumi's eyes grew as large as peeled pears.

"He didn't steal it," said Key. "Uncle Lumi's had that ostrich forever and ever."

The captain laughed unpleasantly. "I thought the girl said it was his *new* ostrich."

Begonia leaned against the ostrich for comfort. The brainless bird had none to offer.

"You two think you're clever, don't you?" he said. "Now, what sounds more logical to you? That a big exotic bird like this thing should belong to a famous traveling circus? Or to three of the shabbiest ruffians as have ever soiled the empire? You tell me."

He was right. Oh, that villainous Poka! No one would believe the ostrich wasn't his.

"I don't know about logical," she said stoutly, "but that's my uncle's bird. Shabby or no."

Lumi kicked the foot that Begonia still clung to. His face contorted into a scowl of revulsion. He leaned over and whispered to Begonia. "How dare you touch me?"

She was stunned. "Why . . . I . . ."

"The new chancellor isn't going to tolerate your kind," the captain went on. "He's just what the empire needs. The old one was too soft. Soft on crime, soft on justice. Soft on letting riffraff like you three roam about. Clean things up! That's what the new chancellor will do."

A strange look came over Lumi. Begonia thought perhaps he was turning green, but maybe that was only the forest leaves.

"What do you mean?" He licked his dry lips. "What new chancellor?"

"Duke Baxa," the captain said. "He's got the power now. The old chancellor ran the empire ever since the old emperor died. But now we've got one who knows what to do with power." He smiled. "Everyone knows the young emperor can't lead a children's parade, much less a mighty realm." The other soldiers laughed loudly.

Lumi's face went pale. "What have they done with the old chancellor?"

The captain shrugged. "Who knows? Who cares! Maybe he died, the old fossil."

Begonia wouldn't have believed it possible, but something almost like concern seemed to pass over Lumi's face.

Then that face grew purple with rage. He tumbled backward off his ostrich and landed rump-first in the soft moss of the forest floor. Probably not how he meant to land, but he scrambled proudly to his feet.

"Arrest me, then," he said, "and take me to this new chancellor."

Key's mouth dropped open. Begonia nearly fell over. But she recovered her wits.

"Uncle Lumi! Uncle Lumi!" she wailed, hoping it was convincing. "Don't leave us! Why would you let these men arrest you when you *know you're innocent?*"

He waved a hand at Begonia. "My reasons are my reasons. Go home."

"What about your ostrich?" asked Key as the soldiers tied Lumi's wrists and ankles.

"Oh. Yes." Lumi cleared his throat. "Hear me, men-at-arms. This ostrich—ow! Not so tight, you great goons!—has become quite valuable to me. I want it brought also to the new *chancellor.*" He ground his teeth on the word, until one of the soldiers stuffed a greasy gag into his mouth and tied a rag over it.

"That'll shut him up for a while." A soldier hoisted him

easily up over the back of his horse. He flung him there face-down, as though he were a sack of wheat. "The new chancellor will see you when he's good and ready." He snickered. "Perhaps in a decade or two."

At this, Lumi's eyes flew wide open in panic. He jerked upward and tried to slide off the horse, but he failed. He made desperate noises in the back of his mouth, looking wildly at Begonia and Key, but the gag prevented him from saying anything.

The soldiers mounted their horses and nudged them back toward the road. They were almost gone when the last of them paused.

"Sir? Shouldn't we return that carnival man's, er, postrich?"

"Let him find his own whatever-it's-called," came the captain's distant reply.

Key and Begonia were left alone in the small clearing.

"What did Lumi do that for?" Begonia's words burst from her. "Here we were, trying to help him, and he treated us so rudely!"

"That's just Lumi for you," Key said. "Begonia . . . ?"

"Why on earth would he *ask* to be arrested?" she went on. "He's an imbecile! A nitwit! I don't care if he's old enough to grow those ludicrous mustaches. He's a spoiled baby, and he doesn't deserve our help."

"A pointed assessment of his character," Key said, "and one that I would find fascinating at any other time, I assure you. But first, let me say this: the animals are gone again."

She jumped and searched for any sign of the errant ostrich and his love-struck cow, but once again they were gone, gone, gone.

She sat down heavily on a fallen log. "Why does everything bad have to happen to me?" she moaned. "Why can't I just find my cow and go home?"

Key sat down beside her.

"Not to split hairs," said Key, "but the prize for the Worst Thing Happening To You was just given to Lumi, I think."

"He deserved it," she muttered darkly.

"Undoubtedly." He patted her shoulder. "Cheer up. With a Finder of Things That Are Lost at your side, we'll locate the animals in no time. We'll just follow their tracks."

"Too late," came a booming voice from behind them.

The world went dark. Rough, scratchy burlap dragged across Begonia's skin and blotted out the sun. Merciless arms seized her around her waist. She tore and pushed and fought at the sack that had been thrown over her, but her captor was too strong. She screamed, and when she paused to fill her lungs, she heard Key beside her doing the same thing.

Begonia's kidnapper threw her over his shoulder and strode off through the woods. Her mind raced. What would happen? Poor Key! Poor Mumsy and Peony, never knowing her fate!

She strained to see anything through the woven cloth of the sack. She could make out some light, and by squinting she was able to see, faintly, the blurry forest floor slide by. Then brighter light and solid gray underfoot told her that they'd reached the road. Whoever it was that carried her set her down on her feet, but she was so wobbly she nearly fell.

Strange hands yanked the burlap sack off her head. She blinked in the bright sunlight. Key stood there, too, with his hair sticking straight up. On either side of them stood brawny men, dressed in grimy smocks and short pants. Before them was an enclosed wagon, painted green with red letters, and iron bars in every window.

"You nearly cost me my postrich," Poka's voice said.

They turned. There he was, shiny boots, red trousers, oily face, and all. The smile curling around his head wasn't friendly at all now. Beside him were the legs and body of Lumi's ostrich, but no head. Begonia gasped. What had they done? Then she saw that the giant bird had a sack over his head also. He was alive, but a prisoner, just as she and Key were. Alfalfa was nowhere in sight.

"Welcome to the circus," said Poka. "This is what happens to people who get in Poka's way. Into the tiger's cage with you."

Begonia screamed. The dirty men seized her and Key by the elbows and bundled them into the cage. She scrabbled, panting with terror until her eyes adjusted to the dim cage and she saw there was no tiger in it.

"Hands off the Maid Begonia, you scoundrels!" cried Key, but the men only laughed.

Poka's teeth gleamed as he spoke. "My tiger tamer was

eaten last week, but you two will do nicely." He leered at them. "Oh, don't worry. There's no tiger in the cage now. He's at the tiger doctor, recovering from his tummy ache, but he'll be back soon."

Stormcloud appeared out of nowhere and shot into the open door like a gray bolt of lightning. Poka whipped out a set of keys and locked them in. Begonia heard the bolt of the lock slam into its socket with a sickening thump.

With a laugh, Poka gestured to the wagon driver, who cracked his whip. The wagon lurched forward, and Begonia and Key toppled to the floor.

20

WHAT A NESTING DUCK MIGHT HAVE SEEN

THE CARNIVAL CARAVAN HEADED OFF SLOWLY down the road. Farther along the beaten path, imperial soldiers on horseback, carrying one forlorn prisoner, traveled at a triumphant trot toward Lotus City and its gleaming palace.

High above the road that had only just been the sight of so many strange doings, a brilliantly colored wood duck swooped down from the sky in a graceful curve to alight upon a tree branch that led straight to the cavity in the tree trunk where his mate had chosen a nest.

Another male alighted upon the very same branch. The colorful drake, if he noticed, did not seem to mind. This male arrival was most definitely not a duck, nor a predator, nor even a bird at all.

A companion appeared at the newcomer's side. A mate? If

he was even watching, the duck couldn't tell. Humans. They all looked the same. But did they usually float in midair? The branch did not bend or sway for either of these arrivals. If the duck had been of a scientific mind, this might have troubled him.

"There you are," the newest arrival chirped in the other's ear. "I've been looking for you. How do matters go today, dearie?"

The male said nothing.

The female took a deep breath. "About yesterday," she said. "I was hasty in my choice of words. I still don't think you should have tangled with my Begonia. But I don't like spats between friends. I've come to forgive you."

The male pushed his round spectacles down to the tip of his nose and stared at her over the tops of them.

"This is actually a nice look for you," the female said brightly. "Big spectacles? Blue vest? Braided beard? I like it."

The male human scowled at her. "You look like a wrinkled prune."

She shrugged. "How else should a prune look, I'd like to know?" She elbowed him. "Has your emperor learned his lesson yet?"

No response.

"What's that face for?" she asked. "I'll bet you used to strike terror into the hearts of your enemies on the battlefield just by making a face like that."

The duck's gray-feathered mate quacked at him from deep

within their hidden nest, and he waddled nearer along the limb's length to give her the squirming crayfish he'd caught and brought for her dinner. She crunched it in her bill and gulped it down in an enthusiastic way that brought affectionate pride to the flying father-to-be's heart.

Meanwhile, on the other end of the branch, male-female relations were less cordial.

"Go away," the weightless man in the blue vest told the woman. "I'm busy."

"Doing what?"

"Thinking."

"An important occupation. I recommend it. But tell me, in all earnest, how goes your project? Has intervening helped the emperor grow wiser? Are things looking better in Camellion?"

He made a sort of growling sound. "They would be if it weren't for you."

"*What?*"

"The girl. Her cow. The boy. The cat."

She stuck out her lower lip. "What about them?"

"You find it amusing to send in innocent children and creatures. You put them in harm's way, you know."

The wispy old woman produced a wooden spoon from up her sleeve and smacked the man's wrist with it. "You're the one who sent the ostrich in the first place. Besides, you stubborn old goat, I'm sending help."

"Go help somebody else, please."

"And I'm keeping a close watch over all of them. *Your* little plot looks ready to topple a proud and ancient dynasty and turn Camellion over to the hands of traitors." She forgot about the branch and hovered in midair before the old man's face. The duck, if he'd noticed this, would have wondered where her wings were.

When he made no reply, she rapped his knee with her wooden spoon. "A-*ha*. The whole empire's in peril. Not even you can argue with that."

"He's got to get out of this mess himself." The old man rose. "He's not worthy of the empire if I must do all the rescuing for him."

"But the stakes! Consider the stakes. You'll have others to answer to if the dynasty falls. Especially if it's known that you caused it."

The old man's feet began to vanish, followed by his ankles, his shins, his knees. "It would have fallen anyway, with a toad like him on the throne. If he doesn't rise to this moment and prove himself, then all I've done is hasten the inevitable."

And he was gone. The woman fumed a bit, then noticed the brooding ducks and made a soft cooing quack of greeting before disappearing herself.

But the duck was now fluffing his feathers for his evening rest, nestling down with his well-fed mate. He couldn't be bothered with anything else. Humans and their squabbles meant nothing to him. Not with ducklings on the way.

21

DUNGEONS, AND UNLIKELY FRIENDS

AFTERNOON, IN THE DUNGEONS.

Not that the Imperial Butler could know what hour it was. Neither sun nor moon had ever penetrated the hold of the emperor's fearsome dungeons. Prisoners went mad in the darkness there.

The butler had no idea how long he'd slept deep below the earth. The first thing he felt upon waking was pain.

His whole body ached. He felt as though he'd been pummeled by a herd of gorillas. His hips, his elbows, his back—everything hurt to the touch.

And his head! His head was on fire. Waves of pain, like scorching flames, radiated out from the back of his skull. Thrum, thrum, thrum, keeping time with his barely beating heart.

He tried to open his eyes, but they wouldn't open. He

tried and tried again. What curse could this be? Then he realized: his eyes were open, but the dark was so complete he couldn't tell.

He remembered the night before and his visit to the chancellor's room. The first few steps, being dragged down the palace stairs, until, mercifully, he'd lost consciousness.

If only this could be a bad dream. Was it too late to go home to his family and abandon this folly of a fine life in the palace? Clean clothes and dainty food and elegant shoes?

Yes, it was. Everlastingly too late. And those elegant shoes, he realized, wiggling his toes, must have fallen off when they dragged him down here.

He tried to sit up and felt so dizzy that he almost abandoned the attempt. But after a while, he managed to get his body upright. He felt around with his hands. A cold, gritty floor of packed earth had become his bed, if not his coffin. A few stray bits of straw littered the floor. Something else—small bones? He shuddered. The dried remains of a long-dead rat.

He began to crawl around the floor. He needed to know how big of a space he was in. He came to the soft form of a human body and pulled back in fright. Had he been shut in with a corpse? He listened and realized the corpse made the wheezy sound of labored breathing. Gingerly, he felt the form. Yes, here was a wispy beard, and here, here was the robe, draped over the round belly. They'd put him in the same cell as the chancellor. No sign of his spectacles, though. He'd be blind without them.

Finding him there brought a kernel of comfort to the dejected young butler. At least he wouldn't die alone. But as he poked the chancellor and he didn't wake up, the butler began to worry.

"Chancellor," he whispered. "Chancellor!"

The old man snorted and sniffed the air, then smacked his dry tongue against the roof of his mouth and settled back down into sleep. Well, then. He would probably pull through.

Sounds of distant footsteps froze the butler where he crouched, but curiosity got the better of him, and he crept across the floor in search of where the sound came from. He hit a wall, followed it, and realized it was a corner. His cell was L-shaped. Rounding the corner, he came to a space with a little bit of light, just enough to show a set of black iron bars closing him in and another set of bars a little beyond that. His cell and some other poor soul's.

The palace dungeons. Deep below the earth. Hollowed out centuries ago. He'd never leave them. Never again see the light of day. His whole life stretched before him. He was much too young to rot out the rest of his years this way.

The footsteps were close now, and with them came men's voices and the wavering light of a burning torch. He watched in wonder as a tall, strong man was dragged in, fighting and struggling every step of the way. It took four palace guards to wrestle him into a cell. They were panting by the time they locked his door. He hurled insults after them until they left, taking the light with them.

But not all of it. What little light remained came from a guttering candle on the guard's table down the hall some distance. By its weak orange glow, the butler watched the newcomer sink to the floor and bury his head in his hands. A colossus he may have been, but the captive butler pitied him.

"Are you all right?" he whispered.

The newcomer jerked upright.

"Who's there?"

"Nobody much," answered the butler. He waved his hand in the dimness. "Look. I'm in the cell just opposite yours."

The tall prisoner squinted.

"Your eyes will adjust to the darkness," the butler said. "Why are you in prison?"

His companion's voice was full of woe. "I got married today."

"Ah."

"That wasn't the reason," the tall man said. "I couldn't pay the wedding tax."

The butler scratched his head, then wished he hadn't. It hurt. "What wedding tax?"

"Search me," the man said. "I never heard of it before. What's a youngster like you doing in here?"

Talking to someone took the edge off his headache, just a

little bit. But how to answer this question puzzled him. Why was he here? How could he explain it?

A well of loneliness and self-pity flooded the Imperial Butler's heart. There was no one to miss him, no one to care that he was taken. No one but this new prisoner to hear his tale of woe and mourn with him the cruel injustice of fate.

"Do you work in the palace?" the butler asked.

The man shook his head. "I'm a woodcutter. Call me Tree."

"Is that really your name? Tree?"

Tree shrugged. "If I ever had another one, I don't remember it now."

The butler accepted this explanation. "Call me Butler," he said. "It's what I do. It might as well be my name."

"Good to meet you, Butler," said Tree, "though, if you don't mind my saying so, I'd rather we hadn't met."

"I'm not offended."

"You were saying?" Tree asked.

"Ah. Well, then. I think I arrived in the dungeons last night."

"You *think*?"

"I've been unconscious," the butler explained.

"Oh. Sorry."

"Before last night, I was the Imperial Butler. Meaning, I brought the emperor his milk at night, his juice in the morning, and anything else he wanted to drink throughout the day."

Tree held up a hand. "And his food, right?"

"No. He had six Breakfast Bringers, nine Luncheon Servers, twelve Dinner Presenters, and several Fetchers of Snacks."

Tree frowned. "That's indecent, that is," he said. "It's full-out wicked."

The butler didn't feel like arguing. "It's a job. Anyway, I've been the Imperial Butler. But here's the thing." He lowered his voice to a whisper, just in case. "The emperor has been missing from the palace now for several days."

"Off traveling?" asked Tree.

"No. That's just it. He vanished suddenly in the night. No one knows where or why. Some of the staff believe it's the work of demons."

"Demons," Tree repeated. "Is that what you think?"

The butler frowned. "I wish I knew. Since he's been gone, three nobles have taken over. I hope someone has stopped them by now, but I'm afraid for the empire. They're vicious. They captured the old chancellor and dragged him down here last night. They caught me when I found them doing it. Now one of them, Duke Baxa, I think, has named himself chancellor, and there's no telling what he'll do next."

"Chancellor," murmured Tree. "Something about a new chancellor . . ."

"How's that?" the butler asked.

"The soldiers who arrested me," Tree explained, "said something about a new chancellor that all the soldiers liked, or something like that."

The butler whistled low. "In one day! How did he win them over so fast?" He did some counting on his fingers. "If he wrote the letters last night and sent them out by rider first thing this morning, yes, yes, the nearest army posts could've received word by midmorning. Oh, but he's a cunning one. I'm sure he promised them loads of money to play along. If only the emperor would come back!"

"Do you think he ever will?" asked Tree. "Maybe if he did, he'd pardon me, and I could go home. My new wife, she's awful pretty, and if she is a bit talkative, I've got nothing better to do than listen, have I? And she had a baby." His voice grew soft. "I was going to be a father."

"Shh!" The butler gestured toward the candle. From far beyond it, they heard more approaching footsteps. In time, two guards appeared, each holding a small, drooping young man by one elbow. His clothes were shabby and dark, clinging to his skin. He put up no resistance.

"For a dangerous kidnapper," one of the guards said with a sneer, "you haven't got much spirit."

"Take me to the chancellor," the bedraggled man's hangdog face spoke to the floor.

"Sure we will. Right after you take tea with the emperor," his heckler said.

"Is the old chancellor dead?" the man asked.

The butler sat up a bit straighter in his cell. The old chancellor snorted in his sleep just then, and the butler prayed no one had heard it.

"What do I know?" said the talkative guard. "But it stands to reason, there wouldn't be a new one unless the old geezer had died, now, does it?"

The greasy little man drooped like dirty laundry. With a laugh, his tormentors tossed him effortlessly into a cell. As the newcomer fell, the butler got his first proper look at his face.

"Oh!"

The butler's intake of breath made one of the guards pause. He turned and peered into the butler's cell. The butler quickly stared at the floor.

The guards left. The echoes of their boots on the floor died away.

Tree took hold of the bars of his cell and whispered across the way. "Butler. Why'd you say 'Oh' like that?"

"It's nothing," he told the woodcutter. "I only . . . for a second I thought his face reminded me of someone. It seemed like it was someone I knew, and knew well." He scratched his head once more and again regretted it. "But who? Already I've forgotten. It's the strangest thing." He turned toward the new arrival. "You there," he called. "New fellow. Whom did you kidnap?"

In reply, the man curled himself into a ball and lay down on the floor with his back toward the bars of his cell, and thus toward the butler and Tree. "Leave me alone."

The butler persisted. "It's lonely down here," he called. "Speak. Let us hear your voice. At least we can pass the time in conversation."

They both listened. The newcomer made no sound. Until, that is, they caught the noise of a faint sob and a sniffle.

The butler and Tree looked at each other. The emperor's dungeons made them both want to cry, too. No telling when either of them might give in to the urge.

Silence stretched between them. After a while, the butler gathered a few bits of straw for a pillow. Sleep was now the only escape from the horror of this place and the aches in his limbs. He settled down on one side and tried to get comfortable.

Tree's voice reached him through the darkness. "Is it really true?" he asked. "The emperor's gone, and some greedy villain has taken over the throne?"

He shifted his weight, hoping to find a position that would hurt the least. "It's true," he said. "We need to get out of here. You need to see your wife and baby. I need to tell people what those villains have done."

"Hey, new fellow," Tree called softly into the cage next to his. "Are you here because of that rotten new chancellor, too?"

Boots sounded a third time, just one set, along with the jingling of keys. The guard stationed down the hall, whose candle was their only light, appeared between the cages of the new friends. In one hand he held the bone of a large leg of goose from which he gnawed the last bits of meat.

"No more talking," he barked.

Tree rose to his feet and gazed down at him. His muscles flexed. Even behind bars he made the guard shrink back a bit.

"We were just trying to get acquainted with the new prisoner," Tree said. "Is there a law against that?"

"Yeah," said the guard with all the cockiness a set of iron bars can give the weaker party in a fight. "I make the laws down here. I don't feel like listening to your voices buzzing away like crickets." He tore the last bite of meat from the bone, tossed the goose leg into Tree's cell, and wiped his greasy hands on his shirt. "Anyhow, your new friend over here, all curled up like a worm, is the traitorous scum who kidnapped the emperor."

22

MEETINGS, BUT NOT
THE WISHED-FOR KIND

CHRYSANTHEMUMSY WALKED THE DUSTY roads as if stuck in a bad dream. She kept wondering if she could wake and find herself back home, with Peony *and* Begonia, instead of carrying this baby in her arms and trudging across Camellion, searching for her vanished daughter, in the company of this odd stranger.

The baby, despite the backache he was giving her, she'd grown fond of, and that was a comfort.

The woman talked incessantly. She'd eaten up most of Chrysanthemumsy's food. She let Chrysanthemumsy bear the burden of carrying her solid little son. And she didn't seem anywhere near as fearful for Begonia's safety as Chrysanthemumsy thought she ought to be. Altogether, in her own blithering way, she was a comfort, too.

Her name, she said, was Song.

They had come to the fork in the road where Song said she'd encountered Begonia the day before. They took a gamble and followed the right-hand fork in the road for hours, because that was the way Song had been traveling, in the opposite direction, the day before, and she felt certain that Begonia would've trusted her advice over that of the wood-cutter, now her husband. Anyone with sense would, she said.

They passed through a strange mile or more of countryside that seemed overridden with cats. Not wild, feral cats, but cats accustomed to being pets. At least half a dozen had approached the travelers, rubbed against their ankles, and purred as if to say, "You may take me to your couch by the fire where I belong. Also, did you bring me any milk?"

They came to a small bridge where the road crossed a stream. They decided to follow the stream through the woods because, the woman said, her husband's cottage was not far from where the other road met this stream, and she wanted to take a look at what would have been her new home.

The heat of late afternoon made the air along the stream-bed muggy and oppressive. Any other day, Chrysanthemumsy might have enjoyed a stroll through the woods. Today, Begonia was all she could see—though not on the path before her. Every flicker of sunlight reflecting through stirring spring leaves swelled her hopes, only to dash them again.

In a clearing, Chrysanthemumsy noticed recent footprints in the soft soil. A cow's hooves were easy enough to spot. Alfalfa? What's more, there was a shoe print that might've been Begonia's. Chrysanthemumsy's heart leaped into her throat. Then it sank again and froze with fright. Next to the cow's footprint was one so ghastly it couldn't be real. A long, narrow, monstrous foot with only two frightful, clawed toes. A dragon? A vicious beast that might eat a young girl? Chrysanthemumsy gritted her teeth and forced herself to believe the footprints meant nothing. Begonia and Alfalfa, yes; the freakish creature must've come along later.

But her chattering teeth reminded her that her heart couldn't believe her own little fibs.

They reached the road and turned toward the right, southwest. Before long they came to a cottage that must've been the woodcutter's. Rows of stumps like jagged teeth surrounded the cottage. The path to the front door was strewn with wood chips. No smoke came from the chimney, and no one answered the door.

Song walked around the house and peered in the windows. "It is what it is," she said. They walked on.

"It'll be dark before long," Song said at length. "We'll need a place to sleep."

Chrysanthemumsy felt tears well up in her eyes. "My daughter has no place to sleep. I'll keep walking."

"Here," said Song, "let me take the baby." She took the

infant in her arm and kissed his cheek. "You know," she said, "that cottage is partly mine now. We could go back and find a way in, and we could rest there tonight."

"Thank you." Chrysanthemumsy took a deep breath. "For now, I'll keep walking. If you want to go back, I understand."

Song stayed with her.

Eventually, strange noises met Mumsy's ears, and clouds of dust obscured her view. Chrysanthemumsy's tired legs found new strength. She began to run. Travelers of any kind might mean people who had seen Begonia.

It was a long caravan, heading slowly in the same direction as she. At the rear was a motley group of people—a pair of incredibly tall men and half a dozen astonishingly short people. An enormously fat woman and an impossibly lean one whose skin was covered completely in tattoos. A carnival. A circus. That's what it was. She headed toward the performers until a wiry-looking man belched out a blast of flame, and Chrysanthemumsy decided she'd keep searching until she found a warmer welcome.

She ran on, past caravans filled with exotic animals, and wagons carrying tents, poles, and trunks of costumes. She remembered a carnival passing through Two Windmills when Begonia was a tiny thing. Ah, yes. *Poka's Carnival of Curiosities*, read the gilt lettering on an especially fancy wagon. Elephants, giraffes, seals, and bears poked their heads between bars or out through upper windows. She saw a long-necked bird poke its tiny head through a small door in the roof of its wagon. The tiger's cage caught her notice for a moment, for instead of a savage man-eating beast in the window, she saw the face of a boy, a boy with leaves and twigs stuck in his hair, watching the road pass by. *Poor child*, Chrysanthemumsy thought. *What could he be doing in a cage?* But search as she may, she saw no sign, no trace of her daughter.

Chrysanthemumsy was breathless when she reached the front of the caravan.

"Excuse me," she called to a man in shiny boots, riding a gleaming horse at the head of the enormous train. "I'm looking for my daughter. She's lost. Have you seen a girl? A milkmaid in a blue dress? She was searching for a cow, or perhaps by now she's found it."

The man reined in his horse and gazed down at the woman.

"Why, no," he said sadly. "I'm sorry to tell you, dear lady, that I haven't met this young maiden of which you speak." He wiggled a finger in his ear. "Pardon me. Did you say you were looking for a boy also? A son, perhaps?"

Still huffing and puffing, despite her sinking heart, Chrysanthemumsy shook her head. "I have no son."

"Ah." The man in the shiny boots stroked his chin. "So sad, to lose a child. A loving parent would do anything to get their lost child back, wouldn't they? Pay *any* price?"

She nodded. "Any price I could," she said, "though the ancestors know I haven't got a buckle."

The man's smile vanished. He clucked his tongue against his teeth. "A shame. All the harder for you, then." He twitched his horse's reins. "Time waits for no one, ma'am. I must be moving along. We perform tomorrow in Lotus City for the emperor's birthday."

It was all she could do not to sink into the dust and sob. "Please," she said, "sir, please. If you should meet a girl who's traveling and lost, would you let her know I'm looking for her? And would you give her whatever help you could?"

The man didn't slow his horse, but he doffed his tall hat and placed it over his heart. "You have my word."

She stood there dejectedly as the slow caravan lumbered past her and left her alone. Soon Song and her baby reached her. Song shifted the baby to one hip and placed her free arm over Chrysanthemumsy's shoulders.

"No luck?" she whispered.

The sun was sinking out of sight now, through the trees, and the dome of sky overhead was transitioning through its softest shades of deepening blue. The sounds of the caravan gradually died away.

Then the mother's tears broke free. "Oh, Begonia, where are you?" she called aloud. "Hear me, ancestor spirits! Why can't I find my missing girl?"

As if in answer to her cries, a chiming tone rang through the trees.

Chrysanthemumsy's skin prickled. Had one of her fore-mothers answered her?

The bell chimed again, and tinkled, as if swung gently back and forth in time with a happy tune. Then a musical moo joined the chorus.

"*Alfalfa?*"

She lifted her skirts and ran, calling to her cow, who mooed her homesick moos in return. Chrysanthemumsy hadn't gone far into the woods before she found her beautiful white cow with the flower-shaped spot on her forehead and threw her arms around her neck.

"Oh, Alfalfa, how on earth did you get here?" the anxious mother cried. "And where did you get this bell? Where you are, surely Begonia can't be far behind."

But call and cry out as she might, Begonia never answered. And Alfalfa wasn't in a mood to stay put. She pressed through the forest, following the direction of the road but keeping out of sight among the trees.

"What's your cow doing?" Song caught up to them just then.

"I don't know," said Chrysanthemumsy. She blocked her cow's path. "Come on, Alfalfa. Come with me." But the cow, as if on a mission, veered around her and kept going.

Chrysanthemumsy tugged the cow's bell, heaved against her flank, and bellowed in her ear, but nothing would deter this cow from moving forward.

"Does she always act like this?" asked Song.

Chrysanthemumsy shook her head. "I've never seen her do this before."

"It seems," said Song, "as though she's searching for some-one."

The two women gazed at each other. "Begonia?" whispered Chrysanthemumsy.

Song shrugged. "Who else might it be?"

"Let's follow her, then."

Beams of dying light swung through the trees as they followed Alfalfa's steady tread. She never went to the road, but she stayed close to it. Once, Chrysanthemumsy thought she heard the trumpeting of an elephant from the carnival. Alfalfa was making good time.

"This road leads to Lotus City," said Song. "Perhaps I can find out how my husband is doing. Maybe bring him some food." Her face brightened. "Maybe I can do some work to earn money to pay the marriage tax, and then they'll let him go."

They came into a clearing, where a larger helping of fading light lit up Alfalfa's white hide until she glowed golden. Chrysanthemumsy stroked a hand along the cow's spine.

She paused when her fingers felt something stiff and crusty. In the dying light, she saw it, and her face fell. Song gave her a curious look.

"Blood," Chrysanthemumsy whispered. "Oh, ancestors. Let it not be Begonia's."

Song, perhaps sensing this was a time when tremendous comfort was needed, offered her new friend the best thing she had. "Here," she said. "Take the baby."

Chrysanthemumsy's hands obeyed. But though the baby cooed his sweetest and best for her, her eyes were far away, and her arms shook to the touch.

"I'm *sure* it's not your daughter's blood," said Song.

But she wasn't sure, and Chrysanthemumsy knew it.

23

DISBELIEF, AND
A DARING PROPOSITION

FEW PEOPLE FIND THE SENSATION OF WAKING up to cat hairs tickling the insides of their noses to be a pleasant one. In this regard, Begonia held the majority opinion. But compared with the shocks that followed, waking up to Stormcloud's twitching tail hair up her nose was the best thing that had happened to her since Poka's henchmen threw her into the tiger cage with Key.

The first shock: remembering that, in fact, Poka's men had kidnapped her and locked her in this dark and stinky cage, which now rumbled over bumpy roads in a most uncomfortable way.

The second shock: remembering that Alfalfa was lost once more. Her silly, pretty, impetuous cow. In love with an ostrich! What kind of a cow would fall in love with an ostrich?

Next, remembering that the ostrich was captured, and so was its owner, Lumi, who deserved every bad thing that had happened to him, not only because he was a rotten stinker, but also because he'd actually told the soldiers to arrest him. The nitwit! The imbecile! The nincompoop!

Yet, for all the biting words she could think of to describe him, she couldn't help but feel sorry for Lumi. He was helpless, and helpless creatures, Begonia felt, deserved pity. Wounded birds and so forth. He didn't deserve to be thrown into the emperor's dungeons.

But Lumi was bound for those dungeons, and Begonia, for being naïve enough to try to help him, was bound to work for Poka until she became a tiger's dinner. She'd managed to escape the panthers once. She doubted she'd be so lucky twice. Lumi, come to think of it, was lucky to be sent to the dungeons. At least he wouldn't be eaten there.

What kind of an emperor would keep such dungeons? It seemed that if anyone was thrown in there, they were never seen again. Guilty or not. It was so unspeakably unfair! In Begonia's life up till now, her biggest concerns had been things like weeds in her vegetable beds or hens hiding eggs. Questions about justice and crime and law had never entered her thoughts. She'd been taught, as all children were, to revere the emperor as noble and good and wise. How else could he rule such a great empire as Camellion? Could emperors be cruel and wicked men?

Her biggest shock, in short, was realizing that the world

was not quite the safe, predictable place she'd always assumed it to be back at home with Peony and Mumsy.

Thoughts of Mumsy threatened to make Begonia lose her composure completely. She wiped her eyes on her sleeve and crawled over to the window.

The night was fully dark, but a three-quarter moon swam in the sky overhead, casting a little light through the bars into her cage. In the corner where the pile of straw was the deepest, Key slept with his face pressed against the floor, his derriere pointing high up in the air.

She was ravenously hungry. The breakfast milk she'd drunk was hours ago. She remembered the spicy mustard in her pocket that Madame Mustard-maker had given her. She was hungry enough to stick her finger in the pot and eat a fiery mouthful.

So she did.

But instead of spicy mustard burning her tongue, a warm, smooth taste filled her mouth. Butter and honey, spread thick and dripping off freshly toasted, newly baked bread. A thick slab, with a mug of warm cinnamon milk to wash it down. Her belly felt as contented as a cat in a summer window.

What in the name of the ancestors? Magic mustard, too?

She nearly tipped the pot upward to guzzle it all. Then she remembered Key. He'd be hungry, too. Reluctantly, she corked the pot and tucked it back into the apron for when he woke up. Her fingers brushed her magical map, so she pulled it out and unrolled it. By milky moonlight, she watched and waited patiently to see which way the map gradually, almost imperceptibly, moved. It took an eternity to feel sure, but, finally, there could be no doubt. They were headed west by southwest on a road that led to a dark sprawl of buildings and shapes. A city. At the farthest edge of the map, she saw a grand and elegant building.

The palace. Lotus City.

Not many Two Windmillians had ever laid eyes on the enameled spires and gilded temples of Lotus City. And now Begonia was on her way to the seat of the divine emperor himself. *Surely*, she thought, *there must be a way to break free from this vile Poka's carnival and disappear into the crowds in such a vast city.* And when she did, she swore, she would go speak with the emperor himself, explain what had happened to them, and ask that Lumi be set free.

But the emperor had been kidnapped! Well, if he hadn't returned, she'd find somebody in charge. The new chancellor, for one.

And to think that she'd only left on this journey to find her cow.

Poor Alfalfa.

Poor Sprout, at home and missing her mama cow.

Poor Mumsy, worrying about her daughter.

"I'll be home soon, Mumsy," she whispered. "I promise. I just need to stay away a little bit longer to help a friend." *Some friend*, she thought bitterly. Stormcloud twitched her fluffy tail across Begonia's nose.

The wagon dipped sharply. Begonia nearly fell, only just catching herself. The wagon continued to lurch along at a slow, clumsy pace.

Key rose from his pile of straw. "What happened?"

Begonia watched through the bars. "I think we just went off the road."

They slowed to a stop. Around them they heard voices calling to one another, men unhitching wagons and bringing feed bags and towels to rub down their horses. Begonia and Key pressed their bodies against the walls of their cage, out of view of the barred windows.

"We're stopping for the night, I think," Begonia whispered. "I checked the map. I'm pretty sure we're bound for Lotus City."

Key nodded. "Earlier, while you were sleeping, I heard Poka tell some woman he met along the way that that's where we're going."

A shadow appeared in the barred patch of moonlight on the floor of their cage. The shadow of a man with a wide, round head and a tall hat.

Begonia held her breath. Key snored loudly and gestured for her to do the same.

They waited many tense minutes as the shadows, footsteps, and voices passing back and forth along the caravan slowly died down and finally came to a stop. Still longer they waited. Begonia's neck was stiff, and her eyes had grown heavy once more. A little more sleep, she began to think, would do wonders.

Key, it seemed, had other plans.

"Well, that's it, I think," he said. "Everyone's down for the night and asleep after a tiring day of travel. May they sleep soundly and well. Not that I'm kindly inclined toward them. Not in the least! But it does seem like they're now adrift in the seas of slumber. Wouldn't you say so?"

She shrugged. Key's ramblings only made her tired. "I guess."

"Time then," said Key, crawling toward the door, "to be moving on."

"*What?*"

He looked at her curiously. "Unless, that is, you want to join the circus?" He rummaged through his sack and pulled out a ring containing old keys, short metal tools, and various bent wires. He poked at the lock for only a moment. Begonia heard a click. Key slowly pushed the door open. It squealed on squeaky hinges, and they waited to make sure no one heard. Stormcloud wasn't so cautious. She leaped onto the wet grasses shining in the moonlight below.

Begonia climbed down carefully after the cat, and Key brought up the rear.

They glanced around at the slumbering carnival. Its garish colors were painted blue-black by the night. Its majestic animals had bedded down to the noisy snores peculiar to their kind.

"Now what?" asked Key. "Back to the road?"

"How did you *do* that, Key?"

"Later," he whispered. "Let's go."

Begonia helped Stormcloud perch on her shoulder. "Shouldn't we free Lumi's ostrich?"

Key frowned. "We'd risk getting caught. Would he even come with us?"

The thought of Poka making off with Lumi's monster bird made Begonia's head hot.

"Even if he won't come," she whispered, "we should stick it to Poka, don't you think?"

Key shrugged. "As you like. But there's bound to be trouble."

They tiptoed along the line of wagons, trying to find the ostrich's. They had to peer inside each cage. At one cage, a ferocious eye flew open, and a bloodthirsty growl split the night. It was all Begonia could do not to scream. Stormcloud's tail puffed out as thick as Begonia's arm.

"Just a hungry lion, is all," gasped Key. "Come on. Just a couple more now."

They found the ostrich's cage at last. He lay on the floor with his legs tucked under him and his neck upright. His body looked like a huge brown egg in the dark.

"How can he sleep like that?" whispered Key.

"Who cares?" Begonia replied. "Just get him out."

This was no easy task. Key got through the lock quickly enough, but they both knew the deadly power of those long pink legs and didn't want to risk getting kicked in the belly as their thanks for rescuing him. They whispered and hooted softly to him, but he didn't budge.

"His eyes are open," Key whispered.

"He sleeps with *open eyes*?" She racked her brains. "We've got to lure him out. With what? What does an ostrich want? What matters to a big, dumb bird?"

"Your cow, I think," said Key.

She tugged at his sleeve in the dark. "Great idea, Key!" In low tones, Begonia mooed, doing her best Alfalfa imitation.

The ostrich stirred, and blinked, and rose on powerful legs to his fearsome two-toed feet, struggling to know what to do with his head in the cramped cage.

"It worked!" Key cried softly. "I never would have believed it."

"I'm good at cow sounds," Begonia admitted. "It comes with being a dairymaid."

"Who's there?" a deep voice bellowed from somewhere along the caravan.

"Hurry! Quick!" Key waved frantically at Begonia. She backed away, mooing still more. The ostrich poked his long head out the open door and hesitated. Key scrambled up behind and gave him a push. They both tumbled out in a rush of lanky limbs and feathers.

"Run!" Begonia called to them, bolting toward the road. "*Mooo!*"

"Stop! Thief! Get back here!" cried the angry voice.

Darkness was their only cover, though the moon was bright. Here there were no trees to hide them, only low rolling ground strewn with shrubs and boulders. They stumbled and raced toward the road. A gray bolt of fur shot past Begonia's feet and disappeared into the night. The ostrich, gathering that this was to be a chase, stretched his legs forward and settled into a loping stride that soon left Key and Begonia far behind.

Running in the dark was dangerous business. The ground hid rodent holes and tufts of weeds sure to trip up runners and sprain their ankles. The escapees finally reached the road and found the ostrich there, standing in the middle of the highway, dazed and blinking.

"He probably thinks he's dreaming," Begonia said. "I wonder if I am, myself." She paused to listen for the sound of pursuing feet. Or hooves. Or goodness knew what. Perhaps Poka would unleash the lion to hunt them down.

They heard nothing, so they walked on as quickly as they could.

Begonia turned to Key. "How on earth did you pick the lock to our cage?"

Key waved a modest hand. "Locks are one of my hobbies, you might say. I am no mere Finder of Things That Are Lost and Noticer of Things That Weren't There Before. I am also a Disbeliever in Locks."

She tapped her ear to make sure it still worked. "You're a *what*?"

"Locks can only hold you in if you believe they should," said Key. "It's amazing how many people believe in locks. I choose not to."

Begonia shook her head. "You are the strangest person I've ever met."

"Having the right tools is very helpful," he added, by way of confession. "Besides," he added, "I had plenty of time while you were asleep to experiment with our lock. It was simple, really. They made it to keep tigers in. Not humans with fingers and brains and a bit of a lever."

Stormcloud reappeared and resumed her rightful seat atop Begonia's shoulder. The ostrich began pacing up and down the road, puffing out his neck and hooting.

"They'll find us in no time if he keeps that up," Begonia said. She looked up and down the road, then pointed to the right. "This is the way we were headed, so this road must lead to Lotus City." She pointed to the left. "That means this is the way home."

"You're the boss," said Key. "Which way do we go?"

She sighed. "Poor Alfalfa!" She turned to Key. "We're so close to Lotus City. I think we should try to get Lumi out of prison."

"But your home!" said Key. "Your mother. Won't she be worried?"

His words smote Begonia's conscience. "She will be worried," she admitted. "Terribly. I hate to make it last longer." She stroked Stormcloud's paw. "But I think it would be better to trade a few more hours of Mumsy's worry for the rest of Lumi's entire life."

Key patted her shoulder. "You make progress, Maid Begonia."

"Quit babbling," she snapped. "Who are you to decide if I've made progress or not?"

"As a Noticer of Things That Are Lost," he said, with injured dignity, "I couldn't help noticing you had lost some of your loyalty to a friend back there in the woods. Well, not a friend, perhaps, but a companion. A comrade of the road. But here you are now, taking a great risk to try to rescue that same comrade."

"Thanks, I think," she said. "Now, quit scolding and stop judging me. You make me feel like I'm back in school, with Madame Inkpot rating my penmanship."

They turned to the right and started walking. The ostrich followed. His was not the brain of the operation, and he seemed glad that someone had done the thinking for him.

Moonlight bathed the road in pearl-blue splendor. This was much nicer than being lost in the woods by night. Begonia had never spent so much nighttime outdoors as she had this week. She was beginning to enjoy it. But her thoughts couldn't remain long on nocturnal wonders.

"It's disgraceful what happened to Lumi," she told Key. "I plan to speak to the chancellor about it. Or the emperor. Whoever isn't kidnapped when we arrive."

Key whistled. "Speak to the emperor?"

"If I can. Why not?"

He scratched his leafy head. "It's just . . . I've never heard of people doing that. Leastwise"—he gave her a sidelong look—"I've never heard of anyone living to tell the tale."

Begonia laughed. "What rubbish. What kind of an empire would it be if everyone who talked to the emperor was executed?"

"I don't know," said Key. "It might be, pretty much, the kind of empire we've got."

"If that's who the emperor really is," she said hotly, "then I wish Lumi had kidnapped him. No, Poka. And locked him in the tiger's cage."

"You'll forgive my saying so," said Key, "but even if the emperor should allow you to speak to him, what makes you think he'll consider the opinion of a young girl?"

"Oh, and I suppose you'd be much more persuasive, Mr. Boy?"

Key threw up his hands. "Not that I don't firmly believe," he said hurriedly, "that in this view the emperor's views are abominable. I myself am a Seeker After Young Girls' Opinions. Every chance I get. But I'm unique in that way. A pioneer." He doffed an imaginary hat from his head in gallant fashion. "It goes hand in hand with being a romantic."

Begonia trudged forward with grim determination. "I've been wandering far from home, chasing a cow in love with an ostrich. I've been held at bay in treetops by snarling panthers. I've been kidnapped by a wicked carnival man, and escaped"—she nodded to Key—"with a friend's help. I'm following an ostrich. And I haven't had a proper meal in days." She pounded her fist in her hand. "I'm not scared of the emperor. The emperor had better watch out for *me*."

"Bravo!" cried Key. "So long as you don't die."

"Anyway, thank you, Key, for getting us out," she said. "I'd still be a prisoner without your help." A thought occurred to her. "You've done it! You've rescued me in a heroic way."

He shook his head. "It needs to be in a *romantic* way."

Begonia laughed. "What could be more romantic than a midnight rescue from peril?"

"Hmph."

"I mean it, Key. You've done it. You've fulfilled your quest."

He gave her a long look. "Does that mean you want me to go now?"

Begonia paused. This exasperating person had been a thorn in her side for the better part of two days. Still, he had been helpful. And his company wasn't all bad.

"Not yet," she said slowly.

He smiled. "Good," he said, "because I have a feeling you're going to need a lot more rescuing where you're headed."

24

LOTUS CITY, AND TACKLING INJUSTICE

B EGONIA, KEY, AND THE OSTRICH REACHED Lotus City before dawn. The suburbs outside the city walls still snoozed through the final dreams of morning. Not even the roosters were awake to notice their mighty eight-foot cousin sauntering through the streets.

Long before they'd arrived, Begonia remembered to share a plop of mustard with Key.

"Mmm! Chicken noodle soup!" he had sighed.

She shook her head. "You're crazy. It tastes like honey-buttered toast."

"You have extremely odd notions of what honey-buttered toast tastes like. Perhaps they make it with chicken and onions and noodles in Two Windmills, but not where I come from."

They found a haystack next to a barn near the city walls

and burrowed in for a bit of rest. By the time they woke, the morning sun was high in the sky, and the towers and spires of the emperor's palace glittered in the morning light.

"Time to talk to the emperor. Or the chancellor." Begonia stretched her arms over her head. "Time to make one of them see reason."

"Hmm," said Key. "I wonder." So much golden hay protruded from his hair that it seemed he'd grown a halo. "Not that I don't have the utmost faith in your plan succeeding, but in the spirit of having a fallback plan, just in case you don't change the laws of the empire with one conversation, I think it's time for me to figure out how one gets in and out of the palace dungeons."

They tied a short bit of twine loosely around the ostrich's neck. He didn't like it, but neither did he give them any trouble. They headed for the city gates and saw, to their horror, that Poka's Carnival of Curiosities was setting up tents on a flat stretch of grass in a park just inside. For the emperor's birthday, no doubt. Of course! Today was the day. They bypassed that gate to avoid Poka and company and traveled far around the perimeter of the city until they came to another, less used gate. They entered the city as nonchalantly as they could.

"What are you two doing bringing that creature in here?" demanded a guard.

"Present for the emperor," Begonia stammered.

The guard gave them an odd look, then nodded them in.

The palace crowned the hill whereon Lotus City sat. All the city's avenues climbed toward it, while streets and lanes spiraled around the palace like petals around a rose. But the palace itself! The closer they climbed, the more vast, more beautiful, and more terrifying it seemed. There were towers of carnation pink and arches of daisy yellow. Domes of aquamarine, battlements of tangerine brick, and carved pillars of purest green jade.

"The emperor lives there?" whispered Begonia.

Key's eyes were wide. "So they say."

The sight of two youngsters leading an ostrich by a string attracted stares from passersby. Begonia became painfully aware of how grimy they both were. They wore peasants' clothes, while the citizens of Lotus City wore gleaming garments studded with gold trim and silver filigree. She'd never felt so out of place.

"Come on, Key," she said firmly. "Let's hide this big bird and do what we came for."

They reached the palace walls and saw acres of parks and gardens beyond, leading up to the palace itself. Outside one section of wall they found a gardener's shed. Key popped its lock in no time—it was barely more than a latch—and they lured the ostrich in. The giant bird, who could never be accused of intelligence, went in without protest. Then they made their plans.

"The chancellor, and the emperor, if he's here, are likely still in bed or finishing their breakfast," said Key. He sighed longingly. "Breakfast! Ahem. Let me sniff around the palace to learn how to get to the dungeons. I'd be less conspicuous if I went alone. Would you wait here with our feathered friend until I come back? I don't want you approaching anybody from the palace without my spying on the conversation."

Begonia bristled. "I can talk to them without your help!"

Key nodded. "I know you can. But if anything should happen to you because of it, who is there to know if I'm not around? A Finder of Things That Are Lost is loath to see his own friends go missing! I'll hide in a bush and watch."

"You're good at hiding in bushes," Begonia teased.

He winked. "It's one of my special talents. I am a Communer With Small Foliage. Trust me, I won't get in the way. But we're the only friends either one of us has in this whole city. It may be bright and shiny, but I'm not sure it's kind or fair."

She nodded. "All right. I see your point. I'll wait here."

Key was visibly relieved. "I'll be back in an hour."

Waiting an hour for someone, with nothing whatsoever to do to pass the time, can be torture. Begonia passed the first few minutes by finding a pail in the gardener's shed and filling it at a nearby pump. The poor ostrich was probably terribly thirsty. Begonia certainly was. She guzzled from the waterspout, then brought the bird his drink. He seemed glad to have it.

Then she waited.

And waited.

She began pacing along the palace walls. Just ten feet out, then back. Fifteen, twenty. There could be no harm in stretching her legs. Her explorations led to a gate, and then, just as she was about to head back again, the gate was flung open. She hid behind the open door before anyone could see her there.

Three men emerged in majestic splendor: a tall one with thinning hair, dressed in white; a short one with long, dark, oiled curls, dressed in red; and a bald man who was enormously fat, dressed in blue.

"How do I look?" the tall man asked the other two.

"Regal," said the fat man in blue.

"Elegant," purred the curly-haired man in red.

"Lordly," added Blue.

"Im-perial," suggested Red, kissing his fingertips.

"Fine, fine," muttered the tall man in white. "Greet the city, so forth, so on. Check. Blessings on the people, etc. Check. Cancel the birthday feast, and announce the death of Little Stinkface. The fiend who kidnapped him murdered him, but he's, let's see, yes, the criminal is being hunted down even as we speak." Here his companions sniggered most unpleasantly.

Begonia listened in horror. A kidnapper, hunted down even now? A murderer? And who was Little Stinkface? Could they mean the emperor? What else could they mean?

"Next, schedule the funeral, two days of mourning, and when that's done, you'll present me with the scepter, and then the festivities will begin in earnest. Music, dancing, carousing." He smiled a wicked smile. "And then, Camellion is mine! All hail, Emperor Baxa the Conqueror!"

"A brilliant strategy," murmured Short Red.

"Truly tasteful," added Fat Blue. "No one could ever suggest you were rushing things."

The tall man didn't seem so sure. "Now, where are my remarks? Rudo, what did you do with the parchment?"

Short Red, who was apparently Rudo, pointed to Fat Blue. "You had it last, Hacheming!"

"No, I didn't."

"Yes, you did."

"No, I didn't."

"Enough of this!" cried the man in white. "Both of you, run and look for it. Get back here quickly."

Begonia, watching this conversation, felt her heart sink. The young emperor had, indeed, been murdered. What an awful tragedy. And now this vain, petty man, this Baxa, would be the new emperor, divinely appointed to rule Camellion in justice and grace? Well, if he was in charge now, then justice was his job. Even if he himself seemed like a very unjust person.

She popped out from behind the gate.

"Sir?"

"*Yeagh!*" yelped Baxa. He placed a hand over his heart. "My goodness. Ahem. You startled me, young"—he glanced at her dirty clothes and shoes—"person."

Begonia bowed. "My apologies, oh emperor. You are the emperor now, are you not?"

The man held his head a bit taller. "Yes, I am." He corrected himself. "I'll receive the scepter in a few days, but, yes, by all means, certainly I am the emperor. Will be. Am. Essentially. Yes. There is no other emperor but me."

Odd, thought Begonia. She dropped to her knees. "Might I, oh emperor, tell you something I've seen that affects the empire greatly? Its safety and justice, I mean?"

The thin mustache over the man's upper lip curled strangely. "Something you've seen? Justice?" He glanced back toward the palace. "Out with it, then, quickly."

Should she trust him? Doubt grew inside her. But the snowball had begun to roll down the mountain. There was no stopping it now.

"I'm a dairymaid, Your Greatness, from the village of Two Windmills. Two days ago, I left home in search of my runaway cow."

The emperor frowned. "Yes? So? What have cows to do with me?"

"I found my cow," she explained, "in the company of a very rude person. A small man, with long mustaches, riding on the back of an ostrich."

Baxa's eyes grew wide. "A small man? Rude, with long mustaches?"

Begonia was puzzled. "His mustaches aren't the important part. You see, my cow fell in love with his ostrich, and they wouldn't be separated. So we were forced to travel together for some time. I will be honest, though it may sound cruel, but you'll see why it matters. He was a weak and pathetic person—"

"Wait," he said. "You said your *cow* fell in love with his *ostrich?*" He pressed his fingers into his temples. "Never mind. You were saying . . . Ah. Yes. Weak and pathetic. That's him to perfection. But an *ostrich?*"

"Why, do you know Lumi?" asked Begonia in surprise.

"What? Lumi? Why should I know a Lumi? What kind of ridiculous name is that?"

Begonia watched the soon-to-be emperor with a sinking heart. All those lessons and Praise Hymns, her whole life long, instilling such awe and respect for the divine emperor! He was such a disappointment.

"His name isn't the point," she said firmly, "and neither are his manners."

Baxa ignored her. "It's the ostrich that puzzles me . . ."

"The point is," Begonia said, "he's a person who could barely comb his own hair, much less hurt anyone. But your soldiers came along and arrested him for kidnapping the emperor!"

The would-be emperor leaned in close enough for Begonia to see the yellowish cast of his teeth through his growing smile.

"They *did?*"

"Yes," Begonia cried, growing irritated. "He couldn't have

harmed a mouse, much less an emperor. Don't you see? They arrested the wrong man. From what the soldiers said, it doesn't sound like there's to be a trial. He'll just rot down in the dungeons forever, all because he looks like somebody else, I suppose."

Baxa pressed the tips of his fingers together. He looked positively giddy. "But this is wonderful! Why was I not notified?"

Behind him, Begonia saw the forms of Fat Blue and Short Red come huffing into sight.

"Found it," sang Short Red, waving a rolled-up parchment.

"I told you Rudo had it," said Fat Blue indignantly.

The aspiring conqueror held up a silencing hand.

Begonia was losing, and she knew it, but she had to try. She felt tears begin to prick her eyes. "It isn't fair," she said hotly. "People's lives shouldn't be cut short just because they look like someone's description of somebody else." She wiped her eyes. "They say you're supposed to be a divinely good person, but if you let this kind of thing happen, you're just selfish and mean."

She caught herself. Had she actually said those words? To the most powerful man in the Three Continents? Slowly, she glanced up to see three faces peering down at her, like three vultures gazing down at a dying rat.

"This young maid speaks courageously," Baxa said slowly to his companions. Relief and hope flickered once more in Begonia's heart. "She speaks her mind, and in so doing she informs us of a person, *rude*, *short*, with *long mustaches*, caught by the soldiers for kidnapping the former emperor, may he rest serenely with his ancestors, and carried to our very own dungeons. But she believes he can't have done it, because he *lacks the nerve*."

Slow smiles spread across all the men's faces. The man's words ought to have reassured Begonia. The looks on their faces did anything but that.

"We would speak more with this brave young maid about this matter," he went on, "but time compels us to be elsewhere. My friends, would you escort this young person, in all hospitality, to a comfortable chamber where she can await further audience with us?"

Begonia rose to her feet. "If it's all the same, I'll wait out here," she said. "You see, I have a—"

What she had, the soon-to-be emperor was not to know. Short Red and Fat Blue seized her by the shoulders and dragged her inside the palace before she could try to fight them off.

It wouldn't have mattered if she had.

25

WHERE A COW LEADS,
AND A MOTHER'S PLEA

CHRYSANTHEMUMSY, ALFALFA, SONG, AND
the baby entered Lotus City's gates just as a grand
gathering of citizens seemed to be breaking up.
Crowds were dispersing from a large grassy park just through
the main gate. The city seemed decked out for a party—the
emperor's birthday party, of course!—but the people leaving
the assembly looked bewildered and grief-stricken. Many
were in tears. Tents and banners drooped as though the festival had taken a tragic turn.

Alfalfa found the nearest avenue heading up to the palace
and began to climb. Song lagged somewhat behind with her
child in her arms. Chrysanthemumsy tried asking passersby
if they'd seen her daughter. But what could she say? A girl
with dark hair? Most people had dark hair. A girl in a shabby

blue dress? That was nothing special. Her best hope, it seemed, was to follow the cow.

They hadn't gone far, though, when Alfalfa's white hide attracted the gaze of someone Chrysanthemumsy knew.

"My good woman," said a voice at her side, "I see you've found your lost cow?"

"Oh, it's you," the mother replied. "From the carnival."

"It is, as you observe, I, Poka, proprietor of Poka's Carnival of Curiosities."

"Have you happened to see my daughter since I saw you last?"

He placed his hand over his heart. "Alas, madam, I still haven't laid eyes upon her."

Chrysanthemumsy swallowed her disappointment.

"Have you heard the news?" Poka asked. "About the murder of the emperor, just last night? On the very eve of his birthday?"

"No!"

"It's tragic," the carnival proprietor said. "By law, since there is no heir, the chancellor assumes the throne. He just explained it in a speech."

The chancellor. She remembered the wedding, the soldiers, and the new taxes. "But the new chancellor's terrible," she protested. "Hardfisted and cruel."

Poka cocked his head to one side. "You've met him?"

"No . . ."

"I plan to ask him," Poka said, "if our circus can perform

at his scepter ceremony. Otherwise our trip here, to perform for the former emperor's birthday, was for nothing."

Chrysanthemumsy barely heard him. She feared she had said too much. Just enough, perhaps, about the future emperor to be accused of treason. Somehow she wouldn't put it past this Poka to tell on her if doing so would benefit him.

The carnival proprietor stayed alongside her, though he grew winded by the uphill climb.

"Is there something you want, sir?"

"As it happens," he puffed, "I, too, have lost a beloved creature. Now, don't grieve for me. It's nothing so precious as a child. But my carnival animals are like children to me."

She wished he would leave her alone, but her nature was kind. "I'm so sorry to hear it." Then a frightening thought struck her. "Don't tell me you've lost a lion or a tiger! Ravaging the countryside, where young girls are about"—she stifled a sob—"searching for their lost cows!"

Poka offered her a dotted handkerchief. "My dear, dear lady, I beg you not to trouble yourself on that account! The creature I've lost is nothing near so frightening." He tucked the kerchief back in his purple striped vest when she refused to take it. "I've lost my postrich."

"Your what?"

"My postrich."

Chrysanthemumsy remembered, then, the skinny bird neck she'd seen poking out of one of Poka's wagons. "I think you must mean ostrich," she told the carnival man.

He coughed. "People with less expertise in animals have been known to call them that."

She sighed. "Your giant bird, then."

"Precisely."

"Sir," she said patiently, "I'm sorry to hear it, but I don't see what it has to do with me."

Poka placed a hand over his wounded heart. "You asked me to keep an eye out for your missing daughter. I simply wondered if you might return the favor and look out for my missing postrich." He lowered his voice. "Someone," he whispered, "has stolen him from me."

"Since last night?"

He nodded. "Precisely."

"And you think," she said, "that I might come across this bird of yours?"

He shrugged. "Stranger things have happened. Good morning to you, madam."

He turned and headed back down the hill, leaving Chrysanthemumsy alone at last with gloomy thoughts. The emperor, killed! The chancellor in charge! It was a cruel world. She quickened her pace. She must find Begonia. Nothing seemed safe anymore.

Still Alfalfa wound them up the hill, straight toward the palace. Could Begonia be there?

"Ancestors, *please*," she whispered. "*Lead me to my daughter. Or her to me. I beg you.*"

Their arduous climb led them to the palace gates. Alfalfa didn't stop but turned along the wall. Song, catching up to Chrysanthemumsy, wiped her sweaty forehead and shifted her baby to her other arm. "What's the cow doing?" she panted. "Taking a tour?"

Then the cow stopped, right outside a gardener's shed. Chrysanthemumsy's heart flopped in her chest. Begonia wouldn't be in there. And if she was, it couldn't be good.

With a trembling hand, she opened the shed. Its lock barely even held. Out burst the skinny head and enormous body of an eight-foot bird. At the sight of it, Alfalfa mooed with joy and nuzzled her white head against its feathery body. The bird wrapped its neck and wing around Alfalfa in a gangly embrace.

Song laughed at the sight, but Chrysanthemumsy's head spun. It was so terrifyingly huge up close! And those feet—they *were* the monster tracks she'd seen. What could it all mean? First that unpleasant Poka, jabbering about his stolen "postrich," and then Alfalfa leads them straight to this hidden ostrich. How could she have known it was here? And what did it have to do with Begonia?

She sank to the ground in the welcome shade of thick shrubs along the wall and hid her face between her knees.

Some distance away, a procession of people approached the palace gates. A lordly-looking man in white, and two companions, one in red and the other in blue, approached.

Song joined Chrysanthemumsy between two rhododendron bushes, and together they peered through the leaves at the men and listened.

"Well done, Duke," said the short man in red.

"Don't call me 'duke.' It's 'emperor.'"

"Technically not yet," said the man in blue, who received a snarl in reply. The man in white turned and waved slowly to the dispersing crowds below.

"What a bore," he muttered. "You two, go inside and make sure my lunch is ready. And then,"—he paused, and smiled slowly—"I have many more questions to ask of our latest visitor, about this . . . this *person* the soldiers arrested."

His two companions chuckled, until the man in white prodded them once more to fetch his lunch. They turned and headed for the palace while the emperor-to-be waved and smiled through his teeth at the people below.

"That's the emperor?" whispered Song. "There's no way he's turning twenty-two."

"He's the new chancellor," Chrysanthemumsy said. "The one who made the tax laws that got your bridegroom tossed into jail. He plans to take over the empire."

Song had a hard gleam in her eye. "Should I go kick him in the shins?"

Chrysanthemumsy rose. "No," she said, "I need his help." She hurried toward the man. Never before would she have been so bold, but never before had her daughter been missing.

"Most gracious lord." She bowed. Her words tumbled

out. "I beg you, hear me. My daughter, she is missing. She went searching for the family cow and never came home. I came looking for her, and I found the cow, but not my daughter. I followed the cow, and it led me here to an ostrich. It is very mysterious. Even more odd, there's a man down there, with the carnival, who says someone has stolen his ostrich, and, oh! My lord!" Her tears bubbled to the surface. "Something's terribly wrong. Who could have taken my girl?"

The man in white stared at her in horror as if she had just turned into an ostrich on the spot.

"A daughter, a cow, and an ostrich?" he repeated slowly. "Why ostriches? Why today? And why me?" He shook his head and muttered to himself, "Is there a connection?"

"Yes," Chrysanthemumsy cried, "an ostrich. And a cow, and my daughter. Do you know anything about them?" It seemed as though he might. Hope sprang alive once more.

He wiped imaginary dust off his fingertips. "Why on earth should I?" he answered. "What do you want from me, woman?"

Chrysanthemumsy's gaze fell to his royal feet. "Help to solve this riddle," she whispered. "Searchers, to help me find her. A proclamation, sent from your majesty, requesting anyone with knowledge of my daughter to come forward. Such things would not be done in vain. Please, gracious emperor. Your help is my only hope."

But as the distraught mother talked, his eyes grew harder, more calculating.

"You presume a great deal," he said. "But, as this is the week in which I'll take up the scepter, I am in a gracious humor. And the particulars of your case intrigue me. I, too, am eager to lay this mystery to rest. Would you accompany me into the palace, and after I gather my advisors, we will confer over a plan to help you find your daughter?"

"Oh!" she cried. "Magnanimous ruler! Bless your generosity."

"Yes," he said. "Bless it, indeed. This way."

Her feet were light beneath her as she hurried after him along the path. In her elation, she forgot she was leaving Song, the baby, and the animals behind. So full of hope was her heart that she failed to notice the pavement of the walk, fashioned of polished rose quartz stones fitted together in a pattern of rolling waves. She failed likewise to take in the splendor of the eastern entryway, with its hanging silk tapestries and marble statues. Her mind was only on her daughter.

Which may explain why she also failed to notice, at first, that after the chancellor-cum-emperor showed her into a small room, and bid her wait for him there, he shut her in and locked the door.

26

NEW ALLIES, AND A RESCUER OF IMPRISONED PERSONS

THE SUN WAS A GOOD DEAL HIGHER IN THE sky when Key jogged over to the gardener's shed and collapsed onto the grass.

"Crunching crawfish!" he yelped when he saw a woman playing with a baby on the lawn and Alfalfa cuddling with the ostrich. "Alfalfa the cow! What's she doing here? And who are you?"

The woman watched him curiously. "My name is Song," she said. "You know this cow? I traveled here with a woman who owns this cow, and whose daughter got lost trying to find the cow and bring it home."

"That'll be Begonia," said Key. "She was here an hour ago."

Song brightened, and her baby giggled. "She was? Chrysanthemumsy will be so relieved to hear it! Here. Hold my baby."

Key took the child uncertainly, then smiled at the wee face. The baby had such joyful brown eyes that he couldn't help himself. "But why isn't she here now?" He considered. "You said Chris-umsy. Chris-anthe—" Key gave up. "I think Begonia calls her Mumsy."

"Mumsy," Song repeated. "I like that."

"You said Mumsy is in the capital. But where is she now?" asked Key.

Song's expression grew worried. "I don't know," she said. "She went to speak with the chancellor, who's apparently about to become the emperor, half an hour ago, then followed him into the palace and never returned."

"The chancellor, becoming the emperor . . ." Key rose to his feet. "And you've been waiting here half an hour? But you never saw Begonia come this way? A girl with a pink scarf?"

Song nodded yes, then shook her head no.

Key raked his fingers through his hair. "That Begonia!" he exclaimed. "She promised she wouldn't try to talk to anyone from the palace until I was back from the dungeons. We agreed it was the safest plan. As damsels in distress go, she's a slippery one. I think she's determined *not* to be rescued."

Song interrupted his thoughts. "Have you got a name?"

"Oh," said he. "I'm Key."

"Good to meet you, Key."

"You as well." He brooded. "If Begonia tried to talk to the emperor, or the chancellor, whichever one she can find, she could be anywhere now." He looked sadly at the baby jabbering in his arms. "That means she's most likely in the dungeons."

Song reached for Key's wrist and held it tight. "Are you sure?"

"Pretty sure," he said. "I don't know if the stories are true, but they say that people who address royals and dignitaries without permission often end up there."

"Then Chrysanthemumsy must be down there, too," said Song. "And so's my husband."

"Prancing prawns!" Key whistled. "We've got to get them out of there!"

Song paced. "But how? Nobody ever escapes those dungeons."

Key puffed out his scrawny chest for all he was worth. "You don't know me yet, Madam," he said, "but I'm a Rescuer of Imprisoned Persons, a Disbeliever in Locks, and a Romantic in General."

Song pursed her lips. "Are you, now?"

"I am," said Key. "The reason no one's ever escaped from those dungeons before, begging your pardon, is that no one yet has had my help to do it."

Song watched Key thoughtfully. "You're a strange string bean," she said, "but you just might be able to do something."

Dire though their situation was, Key smiled once more at the baby. He couldn't help it. "I *will* do something, madam. You can count on me."

Song gave him a funny look. "You're pretty nervous, aren't you?"

"Terrified."

"Known this Begonia long?" asked Song.

"I met her two days ago," confessed Key.

Song nodded knowingly. "That's the day I met my husband."

It took Key a moment to realize what she'd said. "Your *husband*? Two days ago you *met* your husband?" His eyes bulged. "You're joking!"

"Not at all." She dusted off her dress. "Well, Key. I'll come with you and help any way I can. I think I have an idea that might help, but to carry it out, *I'm* going to need to hold the baby."

27

THAT WHICH TERRIFIED
A STORK

ATOP THE NARROW PEAK OF THE PALACE'S highest towers, flagpoles reached high into the sky, waving the proud, colorful banners of the dynasty that had ruled Camellion these last eight hundred years. Most creatures, if they had to live close to the sound of those flapping, fluttering flags, would have found it vexing in the extreme, but the stork pair that had chosen to build their heavy nest at the base of those flagpoles didn't mind it. Their fledglings, when they hatched, would be hidden from view to all but the highest-flying predators, and they—the eagles, the kites, the buzzards—were scared off by those waving flags. So long as those flags kept flapping, it was stork paradise.

If Mama Stork was paying attention, she might have seen a human figure sitting cross-legged atop the tower's ledge, with both palms pressed together above his head, looking down on the swirling movements of the pinhead-sized people below.

"Finally, you do your serenity exercises!" said a voice.

Mama Stork, had she looked upward with her graceful beak and supple neck, would've seen the man joined by a small woman.

"You can't hide from me forever, dearie," she said. "I'm catching on. Now I always search for birds."

The man never blinked. His eyes took in the teeming life below, all those little blots of color, as if he could count and name each of them. "I've been busy."

"Well?" The old lady hopped up onto the ledge and balanced daintily on one toe, stretching her other leg high overhead. She looked as graceful, coincidentally, as a stork. "How's your emperor doing? Will he be able to save your dynasty? Restore justice to your empire?"

The man broke his gaze away from Lotus City below. "This isn't about me."

"Ha! Is that so?"

The wind died down, and the flapping flags hung limp against their poles. High overhead, the piercing eye of a soaring Imperial Eagle detected movement as Mama Stork wedged a little stick into the expanding architecture of her nest.

"Listen," the man said, "don't you have a dairymaid to rescue or something? One of your granddaughters?"

"Begonia? She's doing fine."

"I doubt that's what she'd say right now," the old man said. "A prisoner in this very palace! If you hadn't roped her into this business, she'd be planting her potatoes right now. Safe and at home."

"I suppose you built your great name and legacy by staying *safe* and *at home*?"

With a roar, the old man's form transfigured into a red and raging demon, with fiery eyes, vicious fangs, and cruel, twisting horns. He surged upward on a cascade of smoke and flames, and one very confused eagle decided stork wasn't on today's menu. The bird spiraled downward to the safety of the gloved arm of the Keeper of the Imperial Aviary. Mama Stork quaked in her nest and hid her head under her wing.

The woman watched with arms folded across her chest. "That's *one* way to defend the palace," she said. "Am I supposed to be scared?"

Flames shot from his fists. "Will you *ever* stop *pestering* me?"

The woman switched legs and stretched the other one. "Scaring people is no way to solve problems. You treat life like everything's a battlefield."

"*I do not!*" the demon roared, snorting through his huge nostrils.

"Count to twenty," she told him. "Think about ocean waves."

The demon counted. Plumes of smoke rose from his ears with each number. Eventually he sank slowly in midair. His horns curled back into his head, and his fire eyes became, once more, the watery, spectacled eyes of Master Mapmaker. Mama Stork peeked her head out from under her wing. Something bad had happened, but already, she'd forgotten what.

The former demon, now a tired old man, spoke to the woman. "Was there something you wanted?"

She fired a question back. "Can't *you* do something to help these poor souls?"

An air of injured dignity. "I *am* doing something."

"And what might that be?"

The stork squawked. They both turned to look. She had laid an egg. Despite their quarrel, both the man and the woman smiled.

The man looked back at the woman. "I am keeping hope alive."

"Whose?"

"My own, if nothing else. I keep hoping the young tadpole can learn." He sighed. "But maybe I'm a fool."

The old woman beamed. "*Now* we're getting somewhere!" She stretched her legs into a perfect split atop the highest tower. "Does your emperor feel that hope? Can he have learned anything at all?"

He resumed his cross-legged pose and closed his eyes. He breathed in serenity, or tried to. "I confess I do feel some disappointment there."

"Then isn't it time we did a bit more? Shouldn't we go down ourselves?"

A deep inhale. "It may come to that." A slow exhale. "There's no denying, it may." One more breath in, and one more glance at the egg. "But let's give it just a little bit longer, to make absolutely sure."

28

WHISPERED CONVERSATIONS, AND AN UNDERGROUND COMMOTION

AFTERNOON, IN THE PALACE DUNGEONS.

No one there could know that's what time it was, except possibly the guard on duty, who waited impatiently for his replacement. He had a rendezvous that evening, as it happened, at a dance with a young lady he'd met, and the next guard had better not make him late for it. He'd brought with him a shaving razor, a mirror, and an extra candle. As he groomed, the prisoners took advantage of the additional light. Having nothing better to do, they were getting acquainted, by means of proposing disastrous escape plans.

"I know," said Tree. "We call that guard over here and trip him, then reach through the bars and grab his keys. Then we bust outta here!"

"You're highly prone to aggressive measures, young

man," said the old chancellor, revived at last. "Why not try diplomacy? Surely not everyone is under the thumb of that horrid Baxa. I never liked him, by the bye. We could ask the guard to let us speak to his superiors. When they know who we are, they'll be honor-bound to let us out."

"Quiet over there," bleated the guard.

They waited silently for a moment. "No, they wouldn't let us out," whispered Tree. "I don't think there's such a thing as honor down here."

"What do you think, Mr. Mustaches?" the Imperial Butler asked last night's newcomer to their growing brotherhood. But the forlorn, little man sat in the shadows of his cell, watching them but saying nothing. It was as if he were in a trance. A waking nightmare.

"I have the most curious sensation, young man, whenever I look at you," the old chancellor told the newcomer. "As though I should know you, but I can't think how."

The butler piped up. "Me, too!" He shook his head. "He must just have one of those faces you see everywhere, that looks like your cousin, but isn't."

"Not to me, he doesn't," said Tree. "I only see a face that needs a wash. That's saying something, coming from me."

Under ordinary circumstances, a statesman as lofty as the chancellor would have had no occasion to socialize with a butler, who, in his turn, would never have reason to converse with a woodcutter. But prison has a way of bringing high and low together and erasing the distinctions between them.

"I know," said Tree. "We gather all the straw, and our clothes, and we figure out how to light it all on fire."

"Gracious heavens," said the chancellor.

The young butler moaned. "Oh, I could be safe and smelly back on my uncle's farm!"

"No, we could do it," insisted Tree. "If I can just reach something toward that candle over there—maybe my socks, on the end of a stick—I can light it on fire. Then we kindle a fire in my cell, and when they come to put it out, pow! I knock his teeth in."

The chancellor tutted his tongue. "Barbaric."

"But possibly effective," said the butler. "We run the risk of them ignoring the fire, though. We'd have gained nothing and lost our clothes."

"Imagine winter in the dungeons with no clothes," whispered the chancellor in horror. "No, no. It's too risky. We might die in the smoke. If we couldn't get the keys, we could be trapped in an inferno. Alas! If only the true emperor were here. None of this would be happening."

The butler looked up. "You don't mean you think he could have stopped Baxa?"

The old chancellor sighed. "No, probably not."

The strange, silent prisoner looked up at this statement.

"But I doubt Baxa would have staged this takeover if the emperor hadn't vanished," the chancellor went on. "Baxa's nothing but a coward."

Tree scratched his chin. "How does an emperor vanish, anyhow?"

"If only we knew," mourned the butler. His gaze fell upon the quiet prisoner. Was that his chin, quivering?

"I still don't know why the emperor left," the chancellor mused, "nor what mysterious power could have whisked him away. I tell myself it must be that. Otherwise, I'm sure I would have been able to find him. What his poor mother would say to me now! I shudder to think. I promised her I'd look after him." He wiped his eyes.

"If the true emperor were here," the butler moaned, "I'd be clean, well-dressed, well-shod, and properly fed, with nothing more to worry about but bringing him whatever drinks he wished." He laughed drily. "And making sure I didn't upset him, lest he banish or execute me."

"Sounds rotten," said Tree. "I'd take good honest wood-cutting any day over doting on such a rat."

"Oh, he's not a rat," said the chancellor softly. "He's just a boy. Only a handful of years older than our butler, here."

"A 'boy' who's twenty-two and about to gain the scep-ter!" cried Tree indignantly. "When I was twenty-two, I'd been supporting myself for years and built myself a log cabin."

"He would've grown up eventually," said the chancellor sadly. "But it doesn't matter now, because he's gone." There was a catch in his voice. "I'm so afraid he's gone forever."

The newcomer had crawled forward in his cell. He reached a trembling hand out toward the chancellor.

Tree noticed him then. "Hey, you," he said. "*You're* the one who kidnapped the emperor. That's what the guard said. Why'd you do it? What did you do with him?"

"Peace, woodcutter," the chancellor said. "Don't rush to judgment. I don't believe a kidnapper had anything to do with the emperor's disappearance."

The butler took pity and decided to extend an olive branch. "New fellow," said he, "Quiet chap. None of the rest of us here are guilty of what we're charged with—except, I suppose, you, Tree, for you did get married, after all—but as I say, we are quite prepared to believe you are innocent. But you must talk to us. You must tell us your story."

"Quit your quacking!" ordered the guard.

They waited for him to forget about them. Then the chancellor tried once more.

"Young man," he told the odd little prisoner, "whatever you've done, or you haven't done, take heart. Nothing's ever quite as awful as it seems. Well, most things aren't, anyway."

The little prisoner held onto the bars of his cage and watched the face of the old chancellor with eager, fearful eyes.

"It's pointless," said Tree. "Fellow doesn't want to speak. Guilty, no doubt."

The chancellor ignored him. "I've lived a very long time," he said. "Too long, according to Baxa. But in that time, I've seen that things always seem to change eventually. The good things, and the bad. They all change. So keep hope. Every-one can have a new beginning. Especially someone as young as you. We all need new beginnings throughout our lives. There's no shame in that."

The butler could've sworn he saw the glint of a tear streak-ing down the little man's cheek and into his mustaches. Poor fellow.

Finally, the silent prisoner spoke. "But I've . . . done ter-rible things."

"See?" cried the woodcutter. "He admits it. Guilty."

"Quiet, Tree," said the butler. "He speaks!" But wait. Had he heard that voice before? Impossible. Wasn't it?

"And everyone hates me." The prisoner sniffled into his oily sleeve.

The chancellor chuckled. "The times I've heard young-sters say that! It's normal to feel that way. But it's never true. *Everyone* doesn't hate you."

"They might," Tree pointed out.

The butler glared at him.

"I'm just saying it could be true. We don't know."

"But nobody," the prisoner said, "ever makes it out of these dungeons. The . . . The . . ." He struggled to find a word. "The, er, person in charge here. He makes sure of that."

The chancellor stroked his wispy beard. "There *was* a prison breakout some sixty years ago," he said. "A notorious thief found his way out and robbed the palace treasuries. So, you see, one can never say 'never.'"

The butler groaned. Tree sank to the floor of his cell in despair. But the little man kept clutching the bars, watching the chancellor the way a dog watches his master at the supper table.

Moments later, two most unusual sounds were heard in the dungeons: the voice of a woman and the cry of a baby. The prisoners—even the newcomer—all craned their necks to see, though in the dimness, ears were of much more use. By the light of the guard's shaving candle, if the prisoners peered and squinted, they could just make out the shapes.

A woman burst into the guard's station with an angry soldier at her heels. "Get out of here!" he bellowed.

"Oh, please, oh, please, sir!" wailed the woman. "You have to let me see my *husband!*"

"Song?" yelped Tree. "Is it really you?"

The baby screamed in reply, a truly terrifying caterwaul that made both guards clap their hands over their ears.

"Oh, my brokenhearted ch-child without a father!" wailed Song in convulsive sobs. "Here, Sir Guard. Hold my b-b-baby."

Before the guard knew what had happened to him, he found himself the temporary possessor of a solidly built, red-faced, squealing, bellowing, moist young human being. He held it at arm's length and tried to be heard over the noise.

"What do I *do* with it?"

Song's answer pierced any eardrums that had survived her child's performance.

"Give it a kiss on the cheek, the poor mite, for he has no

f-father to love and protect him!" She knelt at the guard's feet and flung her arms around his ankles in supplication.

"If you hurt that baby," roared Tree, "bars or no bars, you'll answer to me!"

The guard's fellow officer, the one who had tried and failed to keep Song from descending into the dungeons, found it easier to scold his comrade than to scold a sobbing mother and her screaming child.

"Put that thing down, Lee, and clear this racket out of here!"

Lee, for that was apparently the unfortunate guard's name, glared indignantly at the other guard. "I can't put it *down*," he said. "You don't put *babies* down. Not on a floor like this."

"Well, make it stop crying, then."

Lee thrust the baby toward the other guard. "*You* make it stop crying."

The other backed away as though Lee were offering him a platter full of plague. "I don't know babies."

"And I do?"

"Poor little orphan!" shrieked Song. "Poor fatherless babe and his poor widowed mother!" She keened like a demon roaming empty highways at midnight. "And all because their father's been sent to the dungeons. Woe, woe, woe is me!"

And so the pandemonium continued. The baby screamed, the mother screamed, the guards took turns yelling at each other. So engrossed were all the prisoners by the performance unfolding before them that they almost failed to notice something much more extraordinary that was going on at the very same time that Song and her baby were whipping the guards into a state of near insanity.

Here is what the prisoners almost, but not quite, failed to see:

A skinny boy, covered head to toe in the darkest dirt so that he almost blended into the blackness of the dungeons, had crept down the stairs behind the second guard. While both guards wrangled with the unruly woman and her child, the boy tiptoed to the lock of the new prisoner's cage.

"*Key?*" whispered the prisoner. "What are you doing here?"

Holding a finger over his lips, the boy pulled from his pocket a string of shiny tools and old keys. He fiddled and tinkered with the lock for what seemed, to the Imperial Butler, like an eternity. Like a thousand eternities. The boy listened. He tested. He probed around the box containing the locking mechanism with long, patient fingers. Just as the butler was sure the lad was doomed to fail, the boy's white teeth flashed in the darkness. He smiled. The bolt slid back. The stranger's door fell open, just an inch.

The new prisoner stuck his head out of the cell. "Did you come back *for me?*"

"Shh!"

In no time at all, the boy went to Tree's lock. The woodcutter watched him in open-mouthed astonishment, but the boy gestured to him with wide circles, pointing toward the guards and his wife, that he should keep up his racket. So he did, hurling insults at the guards in a steady torrent, but his heart wasn't fully in it. His eyes were glued to the boy's nimble fingers. They moved more quickly this time.

"Was a girl brought down into the dungeons today?" the boy breathed. "Or a woman?" The young butler, who'd been watching the boy like a hawk since he first appeared, shook his head. The lad's face fell, but he kept on working.

One more lock to go, and by now the lad was practically an expert. With a shove, a twist, and a flick, he released the bolt that imprisoned the Imperial Butler and the chancellor.

All the doors were open. All the prisoners halted on the verge of action. The guards were still there, shouting at each other and at the woman and her wailing child. What to do?

The boy whispered in Tree's ear. The woodcutter grinned from ear to ear. He nodded.

Then the boy planted himself in plain sight in the lit patch of floor near the one candle. "Now!" he cried.

Many things happened at once.

Song leaped to her feet and snatched her baby away from Lee. The child stopped crying instantly.

The two guards noticed the boy, then bolted for him like two bulls at attack speed.

Before they could reach the boy, a prison cell door swung out and smacked them both in the foreheads. Neither guard enjoyed this experience. Before their eyes stopped rolling and their heads had cleared, they found themselves locked in a cell together, with the impudent boy reaching through the bars to steal their belts and pocket their keys.

"Commendably done, young man," cried the chancellor. "And you, Mr. Tree, showed remarkable agility."

"Yes, well done, Cousin Key," the butler told the skinny youth.

The boy gasped. He stared at the butler with his mouth hanging open. "*Cousin Shoe?* Why aren't you home with the pigs?"

"Why aren't you?" replied the Imperial Butler. "I never thought I'd see you picking locks like a jewel thief."

"I never thought I'd see you rotting in the palace dungeons!" cried Key.

"*Later*," said Tree. He pointed toward his wife, who beckoned frantically for them to follow her up and out. "Family reunions, later. Right now, let's get out of here."

29

DISBELIEF ONCE MORE, AND A SURPRISE ENCOUNTER

WHILE DARKNESS, MAYHEM, AND SABOTAGE roiled in the dungeons deep below, tranquility reigned above in the gilded halls and plushly decorated chambers of the palace royale. Flowers bloomed, fountains trickled, and treasures beyond price or number shone in polished splendor.

Order, perfection, and peace prevailed in every chamber.

Except for one, at least.

The room that held Begonia had been, for over an hour, the site of a mighty struggle.

She had pounded on the door until her knuckles ached.

She had screamed until her throat was raw.

She had toppled chairs in her attempt to pry open barred and bolted windows.

She had never been in such an elegant room in her life. And she'd never felt so trapped.

Stormcloud, by some feline miracle, had stayed at Begonia's feet as the merciless men dragged her in. She now lay draped over Begonia's tired legs on a velvet divan. The kitty's company brought a morsel of comfort, but only just.

That wicked, so-called emperor! That malicious usurper. "Baxa the Conqueror" was nothing more than a grasping tyrant. A bully in fancy clothing, with an army at his command to enforce his cruelties upon a mighty realm. It wasn't right. It wasn't fair. And it was terrifying.

Poor, silly Lumi, stuck forever in the dungeons below. Not even a nincompoop deserved that. And she—would she fare any better? Would she ever see Mumsy's face again?

At the thought of Mumsy, Begonia broke down. These three days away from home felt like three years. All she'd wanted, last week, was to manure her garden, plant her seedlings, and count the new chicks in her henhouse. All she'd wanted three days ago was to find her runaway cow and be home before lunch. All she'd wanted this morning was to right the injustices of the world. And she'd been naïve enough to think she could do it just by talking to an emperor.

Key had asked her to wait by the shed until he returned from investigating the dungeons. He'd be terribly worried to find her gone. Would the animals still be there? Might Poka have recaptured his "postrich?"

Begonia glared at the painted door holding her hostage. Its

brass doorknob, though beautifully carved, was her enemy. Well, not the knob. The lock.

I am a Disbeliever in Locks.

Key's ridiculous statement rang in her ears. She might as well be a Disbeliever in Thunderstorms and stop lightning from sparking in the sky and scaring the farm animals.

Still, that bizarre boy had set them free from Poka's tiger cage.

Should she, perhaps, give disbelieving in locks a try?

She rose, disturbing Stormcloud, and approached the door softly, as though she didn't want it to notice her. She peered through the crack between the door and its frame. There was the bolt. There was no keyhole on this side, but there was a tiny pinhole in the brass casing just below the knob. Much good that would do her.

She jiggled the doorknob gently. The bolt didn't budge. She turned the knob a smidgen until it stopped turning. No change. She ran her fingers through her dusty hair and tried to think of something. Ugh, but she needed a good washing! Her pink scarf dangled limply around her neck. Madame Mustard-Maker had given it to her. What an odd day of gifts that had been.

Gifts.

She reached into her apron and felt around gingerly for the long hairpin, the one given to her by the widowed mother with the baby. She examined its long steel shaft.

"I am a Disbeliever in Locks," she whispered to the empty room.

She poked the hairpin into the minuscule hole in the lock. Nothing happened. She wiggled and twisted it. Still nothing. In a last angry stroke of despair, she jabbed it in hard.

Something moved, and something else clicked. A spring released inside. The bolt flew back. The doorknob now turned easily in Begonia's hand.

She couldn't believe it. No, she disbelieved in it. *Thank you, Key.*

She peered cautiously out the door. No one was in sight. She was fairly certain she could find her way out. Only a couple of turns should lead her to the eastern entryway.

She tiptoed into the hallway. Her feet fell softly on the carpeted floors. She sped up to a stealthy run through corridors leading to freedom. Door after door flashed by her. She slowed when she reached a corner and peered around it carefully.

The door closest to her banged violently. Stormcloud leaped three feet into the air. Begonia jumped as if the banging door were a snarling panther, ready to strike.

The door thumped once more, then something slid down its length to the floor. A faint voice, brokenhearted with grief, slipped through the gap between door and carpet.

"Where's . . . my . . . daughter?"

The butterflies in Begonia's stomach flitted away on rainbow wings. She whipped out her hairpin, disbelieved in the lock, and fell into her mother's arms.

30

REUNIONS, SOME OF WHICH ARE WELCOME

THE IMPERIAL BUTLER, KNOWN TO HIS relatives as Shoe, guided the escapees up the labyrinth of staircases that connected the dungeons to the many servants' chambers and corridors weaving throughout the palace. The emperor's palace managed to be two buildings folded into one: a magnificent dwelling suitable for a divine ruler, and a warren of hidden spaces where servants slept and ate and worked and cooked and hurried things back and forth, back and forth. Kitchens, bedrooms, pumprooms, storage rooms, cheese rooms, pickle rooms, fish rooms, towel rooms, closets upon closets, all were there, though the emperor might never set eyes on them.

"They'll come looking for us before long," warned Shoe. "We've got to hide somewhere where they'd least expect to find us."

The strange prisoner followed Shoe's cousin Key about like a puppy dog. "You came for me?" he kept repeating. "You actually came for me?"

"How do you know this person, cousin Key?" asked Shoe, the Imperial Butler.

"It's a long story," answered Key.

"What's our plan?" puffed the chancellor, whose portly size left him out of breath. "Baxa and his cronies have already won over the army, it seems. What can we hope to do?"

"Who's Baxa?" asked Key.

"Summon the servants," said butler Shoe. "All those loyal to the emperor. That's most of them. Oh! I know! The bedchamber," he whispered. "They'd never think to look for us there."

Servants they met en route joined their growing party. The butler poked his head through a doorway to see if the closest corridor was empty. He pulled his head back in quickly.

"Key," he whispered, "did you say you're looking for a girl and a woman?"

———————◆◇◆———————

Begonia and her mother were close to making their escape from the palace when a door opened and Key burst out like a cannonball.

"Maid Begonia!" he whispered joyfully. "Come with us! This way! Hurry!"

"Who's 'us'?" she demanded. "And where are we goin—oh!"

She found herself, along with her mother, pulled into and swept along a narrow corridor crowded with richly dressed servants. The widow woman with the baby was there, too, and the tall woodcutter. And Lumi! And Key, standing close beside him. Her head spun.

They tumbled into a large, dimly lit room. A servant whom Key introduced as his cousin—his cousin!—Shoe quickly pulled back a few curtains, just enough to admit slivers of light.

Begonia, Key, and Mumsy gaped at what they saw. The beauty of the palace's corridors had not prepared them for a room like this. Statues. Fountains. Lavish furnishings. Crystal chandeliers. It took Begonia several moments to realize that this vast chamber wasn't a museum. It was a *bedroom*. Back home, she and Peony shared a narrow attic bedroom with one small window.

Lumi ignored the splendor. He went straight to Begonia's side. "Maid Begonia," he said—he'd used her name!—"did you come to Lotus City to find *me*?"

Begonia grinned. "Among other things."

"But why?"

"Because you needed us," she told him. "What's happened to you, Lumi? You're acting very strange. Did they torture you in prison?" she asked. "Drop you on your head?"

It was as if he hadn't heard her. "You came because I needed you," he repeated. He offered his hand, awkwardly, as though he'd never done it before. They shook hands.

"Chrysanthemumsy!"

"Song!"

Begonia was flabbergasted to see Mumsy embrace the widow as an old friend.

"You've found your daughter!" cried Song.

"And you've found your husband!" replied Mumsy.

"Wait a minute," she said to Key, who'd joined her side. "Did my mother just say 'husband'?" She stared at Key. "Those two met for the first time two days ago."

Key nodded. "I know."

"You do?" Begonia shook her head.

She turned her gaze toward the sumptuous Imperial Bedchamber, with its silk pillows and brilliant tapestries. There was enough wealth in this room alone to buy up all of Two Windmills and its neighboring villages, too. Stormcloud hopped onto the gigantic bed and clawed the mattress into maximum squooshiness as if she'd always lived in that regal room.

Shoe went to a wall and struck a silver flute with a wooden mallet. Before its pure tone had died away, hidden doors opened and curtains parted as an even greater entourage of servants spilled into the room. Bakers in smocks carrying trays of pastries, and confectioners bearing platters of quivering jellied fruits. A masseuse, laden with smooth massage stones. A priest carrying a fragrant brazier of smoldering incense. Dancers with silk scarves and tambourines. A new butler, with his hair in black braids, bearing a pitcher of lemon-water. Second-and third-assistant butlers bearing ice and glasses. Footmen, servants. Kitchen chefs wielding meat tenderizers and ladles. The Keeper of the Imperial Aviary with a falcon on his shoulder.

"Who struck the chimes?" cried the Imperial Perfumer.

"*Chancellor?*" cried the chef.

"*Butler?*" cried the priest.

"We heard you were dead!" croaked a third-assistant butler. His ice chunks clinked.

Something puzzling was happening with the servants and Lumi, Begonia noticed. Each of them paused when their gaze fell upon him. Paused, frowned, shrugged, and looked away, one after the other. She shook her head, mystified.

The new chief butler set down his pitcher and embraced Shoe with a kiss on both cheeks. "I was afraid Baxa had executed you." He ran a nervous finger along his own neck.

The chief Fetcher of Afternoon Snacks offered a tray of chicken skewers. "Repulsive man. Baxa makes *our* emperor look like a saint." A laugh rippled around the room.

A movement caught Begonia's eye. It was Lumi. While no

one else watched, he took the new butler's pitcher of lemon-water and crept with it, one shuffling footstep at a time, into an adjoining room. A closet, it seemed, from the elegant clothing hanging along the wall. So much for the new Lumi. He must want all the water to himself.

In short order, the prisoners explained what had happened to them, and the servants explained Baxa's doings since he'd locked them away.

"What do we do now?" asked a dancer.

"Baxa has all the soldiers eating out of his hand," said the priest.

"Eating me out of all my stores," cried the chef. "All they want is meat, meat, meat!"

"No appreciation for cream puffs," mourned the baker.

"He's completely tense," said the masseuse. "No flexibility whatsoever."

"Wait a minute." The old chancellor raised his gray head. "Where's the butler?"

"I'm right here!" Shoe laughed.

"Not you," the chancellor replied. "The new one."

They looked around the room. There was no sign of the braided butler. He was gone.

"Treachery," whispered the priest.

"I never liked him," said a laundress. "Oily fellow."

"Where's that other prisoner?" asked Shoe. "'Lumi,' I believe you called him, Key?"

"He seemed like a dodgy fellow," said Tree.

"If they've gone to Baxa, we're dead," cried Shoe.

At the far end of the room, a door clicked shut.

"How well you put things, ex-butler," said a voice from the dim alcove by the door. "I couldn't have said it better myself."

They turned.

Baxa, the false emperor, stepped out of the shadows, flanked by Short Red and Fat Blue. Standing next to him was the newly promoted butler, with a nervous smile on his lips. Spread along the far wall of the room were two dozen soldiers with blades drawn.

"Surround them," said Baxa's gravelly voice. "Throw them all in the dungeons."

31

TOO MANY EMPERORS,
AND A LEMON CUSTARD

SHOUTS, AND A STRUGGLE. WIELDED CHAIRS
and rolling pins. In no time, they were surrounded and
herded into a cluster. Key appeared at Begonia's side and
held her hand. Tree's loud insults quickly died when soldiers
pointed their swords at Song.

"I do enjoy a happy ending," Baxa said. "Everything all
wrapped up tidily. Off to the dungeons with them, guards.
No!" He paused, and tapped his chin. "Come to think of
it, these prisoners are too slippery for dungeons. We needn't
wait for a trial. Go summon the executioner." Short Red—
Count Rudo—slipped away. Chrysanthemumsy pulled Begonia close, and held her tightly.

"Now," said a smug Baxa, "what have we here?" He surveyed his captives. He reminded Begonia of Catnip, when
she cornered a rat in the barn. Then he grew anxious. "There

should be another prisoner," he said. "Is he still in the dungeons? The little man, with the mustaches?"

No one answered.

"He is wanted for the kidnapping and murder of the emperor," barked Baxa. "He must be punished to the fullest extent of the law." He left off ordering them about so as to wipe his sweaty face with a silk handkerchief. "Did he really get away? No matter. We'll find him. Perhaps that's better. Yes. Avoid unpleasant scenes. But we'll find him, and when we do, he'll feel the swift wrath of the law. Very swift. Very soon."

He's afraid of something, Begonia realized. *He's got something to hide.*

Begonia's dislike for Baxa had taken on a deep and scarlet hue during her time locked in a palace room. Now it erupted into flames. Lumi, though he might be a useless boil upon humanity, had come to be *her* useless boil, in a way. Baxa had crossed a line.

"Isn't it strange," she said loudly, "that you should be so keen to punish the emperor's murderer . . ." She took a deep breath and slipped out of Mumsy's embrace. Was she really going to do this? ". . . when his death has made your wildest dreams for power come true?"

Baxa inhaled sharply. Fat Blue leaned over to whisper in his ear.

"*If* he's even dead. But if he's dead, where's the body?" Begonia continued.

"*Begonia*," Mumsy whispered. "*Hush*."

Baxa blinked. "A body will be arranged."

Fat Blue elbowed him.

"The arrangements, I mean, for preparing the body for burial, are nearly complete."

He seemed proud of his recovery, but Begonia saw a few soldiers begin to look puzzled. Nothing could be more dangerous, she realized, than a nervous man with an army.

"Have *any* of you seen a body?" Begonia demanded of the room.

"The missing prisoner killed him." A shrill edge crept into Baxa's voice. "We will hunt him down and punish him for it!"

A nasal voice behind them spoke.

"It would be an achievement far beyond my abilities," the voice said, "to have killed the, uh, the, um . . ."

Begonia turned to see a person emerge from Lumi's closet.

". . . the . . . how do you say . . ."

"The emperor?" Key supplied the word.

"Yes. Precisely," the person said. "Seeing as I am—or rather, I once was, or flattered myself to be, formerly—the, er, that thing which you just said."

The person was Lumi's size. He spoke with Lumi's voice. It *had* to be Lumi. But he looked frightful. A gold circlet rested crookedly on his untidy head. His hair and mustaches were wet and streaming water over his clothes, which were clearly garments of highest quality, but unfastened, untied, and drooping. A disastrous, crooked, bulgy attempt to button a green silk jacket had been abandoned midway through. He had to clutch the fabric around his middle to keep his trousers from sinking to his ankles.

"I've had a deuce of a time with that word of late," Lumi mused. "Vexing."

Baxa's eyes bulged. He sputtered and shook. "You!" he managed to say. "You!"

Lumi found the chancellor. "Are you all right, my Lord Chancellor? Are you badly hurt?"

The chancellor gazed at him quizzically for a moment. He pulled off his spectacles and rubbed them. Then a warm smile lit up his whiskery face. "I'm well enough, and better for seeing you back home, my Lord Emperor."

"Ah!" Lumi beamed. "Do you know me at last, old friend?"

"You're the *emperor?*" Begonia and Key cried out at once. Murmurs of wonder and joy passed through the assembled palace servants.

"Don't be ridiculous!" Baxa forced out a loud, exaggerated laugh. "Of course he's not *the emperor!*" He tried and failed to smile as though this were all a jolly joke. To his companions, he whispered through his teeth, "*He can't be here! Not now! Get him out!*"

"Your Eminence!" Shoe approached Lumi and sank to his knees, followed by the chancellor, who struggled a bit to bend low enough to do reverence.

"Don't be fools," cried Baxa. "Guards, seize that ludicrous impostor and lock him away. How could *he* be the emperor if he *killed* the emperor?"

The guards hesitated.

"Recall who pays you," snarled Baxa.

The priest kissed his hands in a gesture toward Lumi. "I'd rather die with the true emperor," said he, "than live in the service of a false one."

"You won't get to do, either," cried Baxa, "for *I'm* the true emperor, and here comes the executioner. We'll put an end to all this right here, right now."

A huge man dressed all in black entered with Count Rudo, who startled at the sight of Lumi. The executioner had more neck than head, and more muscles than the legal limit, but what frightened Begonia most was the evil gleam of late-afternoon sunlight off the curve of his long-handled ax blade.

"Off with their heads!" Baxa shrieked.

"Long live the true emperor!" repeated the priest.

"But I'm not a true whaddyoucallit." Lumi carried on as though Baxa wasn't there.

But Baxa was there. "He can't even say the word!"

"At least, I'm not a proper one." Lumi's ill-clad arm flapped uselessly at his side. "I don't know how to rule. I can't even dress myself. I can't do much of anything, come to think of it."

"Ha, see?" cried Baxa. "He admits it!"

Lord Hacheming elbowed Baxa once more.

"The only things I ever did as a, you know, that word,

were order iced fruit drinks and have back massages." He gazed wistfully at the masseuse, whose eyes grew red. "Those massages really were something." The masseuse burst into tears. A dancer rubbed her back.

Key whispered in Begonia's ear. "Are you hearing what I'm hearing?"

Begonia shook her head. "I don't trust my eyes or my ears right now."

"These three aren't worthy to lead," Lumi said, "but then, neither am I. I needed peasant children to rescue me from danger"—he turned a sorrowful gaze to Begonia and Key— "and when they did, I treated them abominably." He shook his head in wonder. "Why they came back for me, I'll never know, but I won't forget it."

Key and Begonia exchanged glances, then blushed at the carpet. In some ways, Lumi was easier to deal with when he was being odious.

He wiped dripping water off his nose and addressed the room. "I realize now that I'm pathetic," he said. "But I do have a plan."

"I can't wait to hear it," Baxa said with a sneer.

"The three conspirators must be tried for their crimes. If found guilty, they will be punished fairly. Not in the palace dungeons, for they will be filled in." Lumi looked up. "With . . . straw, would you say, chancellor?"

The old man coughed. "I suggest soil, or gravel, Highness. More solid. More permanent."

"Ah. Yes. Very wise."

"Do you hear him?" Baxa cried. "He's an imbecile!"

"But I now know that I am," said Lumi calmly. "As I say, they shall be tried fairly, and if found guilty, will be sentenced to house arrest, somewhere secure, but civilized." He scratched his soggy scalp. "I'm not sure where that would be."

"How about right here in the palace?" Mumsy's tone had a bite to it.

"What an interesting proposal, good woman," said he. "I'm sorry, we haven't been introduced. Are you the mother of that resourceful young lady?" She nodded and bowed.

Baxa's fingers pressed once more into his temples. "Are we all going *mad*? Guards! Away with that gibbering idiot."

But Lumi wasn't finished. "As I was saying, these three shall receive a fair trial and a just sentence. After that, I . . . I think it would be a good idea for me to search out the wisest minds in all Camellion, and appoint the best among them to advise me. Together, we'll share the duties of"—he snapped his fingers—"that thing you keep saying."

"Emperor," said Key, on cue.

"Thank you. Yes." He turned about and examined his opulent bedroom as though seeing it for the first time. "You know, I think perhaps I should turn most of this palace into a library and museum. The people should be the ones to enjoy all this. Those of us who need to live here can occupy, oh, a tenth of it, wouldn't you say, Butler? The books and art alone are far too valuable to belong to just me." Color came into Lumi's cheeks as his excitement grew. "I know! The parks and menageries could become . . . what do you call them . . . yes, zoological gardens. For all the citizens of Camellion to visit." He smiled, and then his face clouded. "I hope none of the younger children will be eaten by the lions. Are there ways to prevent that, chancellor?"

"I believe so," said that gentleman.

Lumi nodded. "I'm relieved to hear it." Then his expression grew serious. "I expect there will be a great deal of work to do. My travels have shown me that running an empire is not so, er, effortless as I had supposed. Dungeons, justice, crime . . . I have a lot to learn and much to fix." He turned toward Tree and Song. "Our armies, I think, need better pay and more opportunities. Our tax laws need reform, too. A wedding tax? Absurd!"

Tree cheered.

Lumi bowed toward the chancellor. "Old friend, I never appreciated all that you managed to do, until now."

The old man's eyes were bright. "It was my honor, Your Highness."

"Lumi!" Begonia marveled. "What's come over you?"

"Hush," whispered Mumsy. "Let them be."

If the chancellor felt sentimental, Baxa was anything but. "Oh, *please*," cried he. "If you think this sudden change of heart is even remotely real, you're fools, all of you. Enough of this! I've known him for years. I've endured more torture from listening to him prattling on, the selfish, stuck-up pig—more agony from pretending to find his every word brilliant and hilarious—more misery, I tell you, than he'd ever face, rotting a thousand lifetimes in the dungeons."

Begonia cocked her head to one side. "You *do* know him? So he *is* the emperor, then?"

Baxa bared his teeth. "Silence, impudent girl." He turned to the soldiers. "Soldiers, hear me. The old regime is gone. The weak, childish emperor is dead. That's what the people believe, and that's what will soon be the case. *I* pay you now. Keep your silence each of you in this room, and you'll retire tomorrow as wealthy men. Executioner, pick your spot and do your job."

At just that moment, something soft and white exploded across Baxa's face.

It was a powdered sugar cream puff bursting with lemon-custard filling.

From the midst of the circle of prisoners, a jowly confectioner trembled in her spot, with one arm still outstretched, demonstrating excellent throwing form and wrist follow-through.

Time dangled in its place, like a drop of water on an Imperial Bedchamber fountain.

Then the army of servants exploded in a roar of berserk battle rage. Silver trays, golden chalices, massage stones, rolling pins, and jellied quinces pelted the imperial soldiers. The Keeper of the Imperial Aviary's eagle screeched and flapped its mighty wings in the soldiers' faces. With the cry of a wolf leading his pack, Tree entered the fray, bowling soldiers left and right with long tree-chopping limbs. Song screamed, her baby screamed. Two soldiers collapsed onto the Imperial Bed, plugging their ears. Stormcloud didn't like them there, and she let them know it with her claws.

But even the fiercest lemon custard is ultimately no match for a sword. Short Red and Fat Blue skirted around the ruckus and went straight for Lumi. They closed in on him like sharks, and each seized him by an elbow just as the last of the rebels was pinned down by a soldier.

That was when things took a turn for the strange.

The floor beneath them shook. Boots stamped, spear-butts thumped, and shields clanged whilst wall panels around the chamber swiveled, and that elite but nearly forgotten squadron of warriors emerged from their hiding places: the Guards of the Imperial Bedchamber.

Attached to no commander but the emperor, and sworn to protect his person to the death, they had watched in silence through cleverly disguised peepholes until angry hands were laid upon Lumi. The others had not been their concern. But the instant he was threatened, they surrounded Baxa's soldiers and cronies with lightning speed.

Not even they, however, anticipated the mighty help that was on its way.

The main door to the Imperial Bedchamber burst open with a bang. An eight-foot bird pelted through on sinewy legs and tore across the cavernous chamber in a few rapid strides.

Before Short Red Rudo knew what had hit him, a tremendous shove from one of those terrible pink limbs sent him flying through the air, landing facedown on a sofa. Before Fat Blue Hacheming could congratulate himself on a narrow miss, his portly belly met the stampeding forehead of a single-minded milk cow. The cow's forehead won. Hacheming rolled heels over nose into a goldfish pool and stayed there.

"Lightfoot!" cried the Keeper of the Imperial Aviary. "Come to Papa!"

But the ostrich went straight to Lumi and stood huffing and flapping his wings with protective bird rage by the true emperor's side.

A breathless pair of footmen ran into the room and gazed, wide-eyed, at the chaos. "We tried to stop them!" one said, panting. "The beasts kicked and butted the eastern entry doors to bits!"

Lumi waved to the footmen. "It's all right," he told them. "The ostrich and his cow are welcome guests in my private rooms." The footmen left showing no surprise at this statement.

The Captain of the Guards of the Imperial Bedchamber bowed to the emperor. "Shall we take the prisoners to the dungeons, Your Excellence?"

Lumi scratched his nose. "Hmm. I think probably you'd better take them to the kitchens and feed them something. The soldiers can go after that, but give them a good talking-to first. These three—I'd say house arrest in their bedrooms, upstairs, until we can decide what to do next. How does that sound, chancellor?"

"Most gracious and merciful," answered that venerable person. "Possibly too much so," he added in a whisper to Shoe.

A middle-aged servant bowed deeply to Lumi. "Would you like me to draw you a relaxing bath before you prepare for your evening meal, O Exalted One?"

"A bath!" Lumi sighed. "I can't just yet, until these, er, traitors are dealt with, but a bath before bed would be heavenly tonight. If you'd fill it for me, this time, I'd be grateful." Lumi stepped over Baxa's ankles as the bedchamber guards tied his wrists. "After today, I'll try to do it myself. And if you could just give me a small refresher on what one does with soap . . ."

Mumsy slipped her arm around Begonia's waist. "He's truly helpless, isn't he?" she whispered in her daughter's ear.

"Pretty much," Begonia said. "But in his own strange way, he grows on you over time."

32

SQUABBLING VISITORS, AND MATTERS INVOLVING NAMES

THE TRAITORS WERE TAKEN OFF TO BE LOCKED in their rooms, and Baxa's soldiers trudged off to the palace kitchens for a dinner of fish soup and crusty bread served with a steaming plop of guilty remorse, while the servants filed out to return to their duties. The keeper of the aviary returned to his remaining birds.

The rest of the group dissolved into puddles of exhaustion. Tree and Song curled up on a couch, oblivious to all else, while the baby slept in Song's arms. The chancellor sat down. Shoe, the butler, flopped facedown in a giant cushion and began to snore. Chrysanthemumsy led Begonia to a sofa, where she began stroking her daughter's hair. Alfalfa and Lightfoot stood ankle-deep in one of the fishponds, with Lightfoot blinking at the room at large and Alfalfa blinking coyly at her tall, handsome bird-beau. Emperor Lumi sank into a soft chair and stretched out his feet with a moan of relief. After all the chaos and danger, a moment of peaceful silence was bliss.

But it was not to last. Voices, seemingly coming from the ceiling, pierced the stillness.

". . . *told* you I had it all under control."

"Pigeon feathers! You made a colossal bungle of it all. It was my cow that saved everything."

Begonia, Mumsy, Lumi, and Key scanned the room for the owners of the voices.

"Your cow!" sputtered the first voice. It sounded like an older man. "My ostrich is the true hero."

"Begonia," whispered Key. "What's going on?"

"Mumsy," whispered Begonia, "those voices sound just like . . ."

Mumsy placed a finger over her lips, and nodded. *Master Mapmaker*, she mouthed silently. *Madame Mustard-maker.*

"But how?" whispered Begonia.

They waited, but the voices had gone silent.

"Now you've done it," grumbled Master Mapmaker's voice. "They heard us."

"I? I haven't done anything. And if you can't keep your voice down, you've got no one but yourself to blame."

"Look!" Begonia whispered. She pointed toward a gilt chandelier. Two shadowy figures seemed to hover behind its ornate lamps, jabbing fingers toward each other in a full-out spat. Realizing the people in the room were staring at them, they froze, mid-jab.

"They *see* us!" the woman's voice hissed.

"Madame Mustard-maker!" Begonia cried. "How did you get in here?" She gulped. "I mean, up there?"

The old woman peeked out from behind the chandelier, then descended in a flutter of scarves. Her face crinkled with pleasure. "I'm here and I'm there, child. How nice of you to remember me."

"But *why* are you here?" She blinked. "And how were you . . . up *there*?" Then the impossible, unthinkable truth became obvious. "You're . . . an immortal? *An ancestor?*"

"Right as rhubarb," the woman said. "Not, as some have said, 'just a bunch of stories.'"

Begonia went down upon one shaky knee. That was what she'd told Key not long ago.

"And . . . Master Mapmaker?" Begonia inquired. "Why are *you* here?"

"Taking stock of the damage he's caused," said Madame Mustard-maker.

An old man with a gray braided beard hanging down his blue-vested belly floated downward, landing next to a harp.

"There wouldn't have been damage," he cried, "if you hadn't barged in."

"Without my help, this charade would've ended in ruin!"

Madame Mustard-maker winked at Begonia. "We're old friends. *Very* old friends."

"Do you know these persons?" Lumi asked Chrysanthe-mumsy.

Begonia's mother wrapped an arm around her daughter. "I thought they were from Two Windmills," she said. "Now, I don't know what to think."

Master Mapmaker addressed Lumi. "Do you remember me?"

Lumi nearly dropped his droopy pants. "Should I?"

The mapmaker snapped his fingers. In a puff of smoke, he vanished. A scaly red creature appeared in his place, with curving horns, cruel teeth, and devil's eyes, hovering high in a pillar of fire. He arched his back and roared. "*Cower before me, mortal!*"

"He's come back for me!" Lumi shrieked. He dove behind his ostrich, who hissed at the apparition.

"A demon!" cried Key. He threw himself in front of Begonia.

"*Now do you remember me, quisling emperor?*" The voice sounded like final doom.

"Save me! Make him go away!" cried Lumi.

"Oh, stop it, you great bully," Madame Mustard-maker told the demon. She hopped down from her perch and yanked on the demon's pointy tail. "'*Cower before me*'? Pathetic! You're no better than he was, you know that? You're two yolks in the same egg."

The demon vanished, leaving the mapmaker in his place. "That," he told Lumi's posterior, which was all of him that could be seen at the moment, "is how I looked when last we spoke."

"Is he gone?" wailed Lumi.

"He was a bully, you're a bully," scolded Madame Mustard-maker. "He was a tyrant, you're a tyrant. He had a beastly temper, and you're no better."

"Pig slop!" Master Mapmaker pointed an accusing finger toward Lumi. "He's a coward with a spine of orange jelly. I was never like that."

"Is that so?" Madame Mustard-maker waved a wooden spoon in his face. "That's not what I heard. When you were alive, your exploits at the Battle of Rees were praised to the skies! Set to music! Painted on porcelain pots! But later on, in the Heavenly Hall of the Ancestors, I met eye-witnesses who sang a very different tune. About a certain young emperor, cringing in the supply tents until the enemy army had the misfortune to blow up their own powder wagon."

Master Mapmaker's face puffed a brilliant shade of orange. "Who told you that?"

Lumi's narrow face poked out from under Lightfoot.

The chancellor spoke. "Do you mean to say . . . you're *Emperor Gowli the First?*"

Master Mapmaker said nothing. Behind his back, Madame Mustard-maker winked.

"My . . . let me see . . ." Lumi used his fingers. "My great-great-great-great-grandfather?"

Master Mapmaker stared at him piercingly.

Lumi pointed indignantly toward a wall. "That tapestry depicts you winning the Battle of Rees in great triumph and glory!"

"Fibs," Madame Mustard-maker whispered loudly.

"Will you be quiet?" roared Master Mapmaker. "Ahem. In my life, I was Emperor Gowli, yes. But now you may call me Grandfather Spirit."

Madame Mustard-maker beamed. "And I'm Grandmother Spirit."

"You're married?" asked Key.

Grandfather Spirit's face wrinkled as though he'd bitten a lemon.

"Marriage isn't part of our lives now, dearie," said Grandmother Spirit. "Grandfather Spirit and I met at Games Night in the Heavenly Hall of the Ancestors."

Begonia stood up. "Will somebody please explain?" she cried. "We've known you both for years as Master Mapmaker and Madame Mustard-maker. Now you're venerable ancestor spirits?"

"Not exactly, my sweet," said Grandmother Spirit. "We are, yes. But your mapmaker and mustard-maker are still back in your village, making their maps and mixing their sauces. We just . . . borrowed them a bit. Their appearances, that is. Not their bodies! Heavens. Not that."

Begonia pointed to Grandfather Spirit. "Does our map-maker make magic maps?"

"All maps are magical," Grandfather Spirit said, "but I gave your map a little extra help." He coughed. "Once I saw *she'd* roped you into this"—gesturing toward Grandmother Spirit—"I knew you'd need help to find your way home. She leads people on wild-ostrich chases."

Lightfoot the ostrich wandered over to Grandfather Spirit and hooted at him.

"Well done, well done, my fine fellow," Grandfather Spirit told him, and stroked his neck.

Alfalfa meandered over to Grandmother Spirit, lowing softly. Grandmother Spirit scratched behind the cow's ears. "That's a good girl! I *knew* you could save the empire."

"We've been through this," Grandfather Spirit said through gritted teeth. "Your cow didn't—"

"*Her* cow?" cried Mumsy. "That's *our* cow. Make her stop following that bird!"

Grandmother Spirit waggled a finger at Mumsy. "I never interfere with true love, dear. Not once it's gotten going." She gave her chin a thoughtful tap with her wooden spoon. "I have been known to give it a helpful starting nudge or two . . ."

Servants began bringing in trays of fruits, vegetables, savories, cheeses, dainties, and sweets. Key dove across two plush chairs to be the first at the impromptu buffet.

Lumi hitched his trousers. "What was all this about?" he

cried. "Why did you do this? Terrorize me as a demon! Banish me! Make the people who know me best unable to recognize my face, or my voice! Gum up my mouth so I couldn't say my title, my name, or my home to anyone! Why would you be so hateful to me?"

Grandfather Spirit plucked the harp. "Don't you know, son?"

"To save the empire," supplied Grandmother Spirit.

"From what?" cried Lumi.

Grandfather Spirit thumped him in the chest with his forefinger. "From *you!* The biggest crybaby ever to sit on the throne of Camellion! No courage, no kindness, no feeling for others whatsoever. The most selfish, spoiled, stuck-up—"

"All right," Lumi stammered. "I had some lessons to learn. But the empire was running fine before you kicked me out! You could've killed me!"

Grandfather Spirit became a roaring red demon once more. "*But I didn't, did I?*"

"But what if you had?" demanded Lumi. "I nearly broke my neck jumping out that window to get away from you!"

Smoke poured from the demon's ears. "I sent the ostrich to catch you and protect you, you nitwit!"

"Ostriches are the stupidest creatures on two legs!" cried Begonia.

"That's debatable," said Grandmother Spirit. "I've known stupider creatures on two legs. Some of them courted me.

But you're right, my dear, you're right, absolutely. It was a reckless, foolhardy plan. So I fixed it all by sending Alfalfa to the rescue."

"A *cow?*" cried Mumsy. "You sent our milk cow to save the empire?"

"I don't see what all the fuss is about," said Grandmother Spirit. She took a celery stick from the refreshment tray and crunched into it. "How else was I to send Begonia to save the emperor without causing Alfalfa to fall in love with Lightfoot, and vice versa?"

"But Alfalfa had never even *met* Lightfoot!" Begonia realized how silly that sounded.

Grandmother Spirit smiled. "In my day, dear, we were partial to arranged marriages. A simple love charm was all it took. But sometimes, all you need to do is meet." She winked at Tree and Song, who had both fallen asleep on the couch, with the baby nestled in Song's arms. "And then, you just know."

"Applesauce!" Mumsy covered Begonia's ears. "Don't fill my daughter's head with nonsense. And shame on you! Begonia's young. She should be home with her mother!"

"See?" Grandmother Spirit took another bite of celery. "If I'd asked your permission, you would've said no. So I had to send the cow."

"That's kidnapping," cried Mumsy.

"*Borrowing,*" said Grandmother Spirit.

"Weren't you ever a mother?"

"I had every intention of giving her back."

Key licked sauce off his fingers. "Excuse me," he said. "Which of you sent me to help?"

Grandmother Spirit and Grandfather Spirit looked at each other briefly, then shook their heads.

"You, young man," said Grandfather Spirit, "weren't in our plans."

Key's face fell.

"You were a bonus," Begonia said stoutly. Key's grin filled the room, and his slouch transformed into a tall, proud strut. Much like Lightfoot. *Uh-oh*, thought Begonia.

Chrysanthemumsy rose wearily. "Come on, Begonia," she said. "Let's find a place to sleep. In the morning, we'll go home." She nodded to Grandmother Spirit. "You won't free Alfalfa from this strange affection for the ostrich?"

"True love." Grandmother Spirit spread her hands wide. "My hands are tied."

"Then you're a cow thief," Mumsy muttered.

"*Borrowing*," sang Grandmother Spirit.

"Hmph."

While the mother and the grandmother spirit squabbled, Lumi sat down on the bed next to Stormcloud and tentatively reached out to pet her. She flicked her tail, then looked away, but allowed him to stroke her soft gray fur.

"I never knew you liked cats, Lumi," Begonia said.

Grandmother Spirit's ears caught this. "One can't afford not to like cats," she warned, "and you'd do well to remember that, young man. Emperors need all the luck they can get, and cats are the luckiest creatures I know. Well, perhaps next to ostriches and cows."

Lumi looked up from the purring kitty. "I'm sorry to deprive you of your cow, madam," he told Mumsy. "If I may, I'd like to give you a cow with a calf. Then you'll have to come back for a visit, to reunite Alfalfa's calf with her mother." He looked hesitantly at Begonia. "Perhaps you would like to pay a visit to the menagerie when you return?"

Begonia curtseyed. "I'd like that." Then she paused. "Does it have any panthers?"

Lumi smiled. It changed his appearance so completely that Begonia took a step back.

"Lumi," she said, "I think you will learn to be a good emperor."

He bit his lip. "I hope so," he said quietly. "But I'm afraid."

"Don't be. You can do it," she said. She grinned. "You're nothing like the selfish brat you were when we first met you."

"But what if, when they give me the scepter, I become that person again?" Lumi asked.

Grandmother Spirit elbowed Grandfather Spirit. "Listen to that," she cooed. "He's *learning*, the dear boy. He'll make you proud yet." Grandfather Spirit rolled his eyes.

An idea fizzed into Begonia's brain. "Keep Key close at hand," she suggested. Key looked up from the refreshment table with a clump of noodles dangling from his mouth that wiggled like a sea creature. "He's a Reminder of The Kind of

Person One Wants to Be. And besides," she said, "you have a new opening in your staff of butlers. His cousin can train him." They glanced over at Shoe, the Imperial Butler, snoring facedown on a cushion.

She turned again to the once and future emperor. "Lumi," she said. "I mean, Your Emperor-ness. You said you weren't allowed to reveal your name. Isn't Lumi your name?"

Lumi looked away. "In a way. But not really."

"His name," said Grandfather Spirit sternly, "is Emperor Gowli the Seventh."

"*Ohhh*," Begonia said slowly. "I see."

"My mother called me Lumi when I was very young," said Emperor Gowli the Seventh.

"Why?" asked Key.

The emperor stared at his toes. "It's short for Luminous Child of Heavenly Perfections."

Begonia decided to be kind. "That's very sweet. I'm sure you were." She reached for a cherry tart. "And it explains a lot."

And that's when Poka walked into the room.

33

A COMIC PERFORMANCE, AND A FAREWELL TO THE CARNIVAL

An assistant butler ushered him into the Imperial Bedchamber.

"Mr. Poka, of Poka's Carnival of Curiosities, begs audience with the emperor."

"Greetings, folks and carnival-goers," Poka said, "I was told I could find the emperor here." He gasped. "My postrich!"

"*You!*" cried Begonia.

Poka headed straight for Lightfoot. "Thank you, noble friends, for finding my beautiful bird for me! Our carnival isn't complete without him."

"Why, you lying thief!" Begonia cried. "That's Lumi's ostrich!"

Poka saw Begonia then, and recognition flashed across his face. He composed himself quickly, and smiled indulgently at Begonia. "This is my niece," he explained to the room at large. "She's a bit . . . deranged. Unstable. But I've looked after her, poor thing, ever since her parents died when she was a baby."

"Liar!" cried Key. "We'd never met him before yesterday. He kidnapped us both."

Poka searched the room for someone who looked as though they were in charge. He settled on the chancellor.

"Sir," he said, "my carnival came to Lotus City to perform for the former emperor's birthday, may he rest in blessed harmony with his ancestors. I've come to offer the exalted *new* chancellor—that is, emperor, very soon—a special carnival performance for his upcoming scepter ceremony."

The chancellor's eyes twinkled. He looked to Lumi, who folded his arms across his chest, only just remembering in the nick of time that he needed at least one hand to hold up his trousers. The sneer on his face reminded Begonia of the Lumi she'd first met in the woods. "There's been a change of plans," Lumi informed Poka. "No carnival will be desired at today's festivities."

Poka recognized Lumi then. He squealed and ran around behind Master Mapmaker, using his body as a shield.

"Venerable elder," he cried, "save me from that dangerous person! It is he who stole my postrich from me. He's the one who kidnapped and murdered the emperor!"

"You don't say!" Grandmother Spirit's eyes twinkled. "Here. Try a taste of my mustard."

"*Mmph!*" Poka's reply was muffled by a large wooden

spoon of mustard poked into his mouth. Then the spices hit his tongue, and he began hopping about in agony. "Hoo! Hah! Owwowow! Wah—wah—water!"

Alfalfa nudged him, and he landed hard on the seat of his bright red trousers in a goldfish pool. Still panting, he plunged his face, tall hat and all, into the water.

"That's the pool the animals drank from," Key whispered to Begonia. She giggled.

Poka staggered to his feet. Water streamed down his face, over his striped waistcoat, and down his legs, filling his shiny boots. He glared at Begonia and Key's laughter.

"Rest assured," he said darkly, "that the new emperor will be informed of the insulting way I was treated by each of you."

Lumi nodded. "I'm sure the emperor—Oh! I said it!—will avenge you swiftly."

"Well done. You said 'emperor.' Idiot!" Poka sneered. "My postrich and I are leaving." With a speed Begonia wouldn't have guessed he could muster, Poka pulled a leather leash from his pocket, clipped it around Lightfoot's neck, and tugged him halfway across the room.

"*Hands off him!*" screamed Lumi. He took a running start and jumped, his arms and legs clawing the air. "*That's—my—BIRD!*" With each word he bounced from one springy couch to another, vaulting the room until—and Begonia wouldn't have believed it if she hadn't seen it—he landed, kersplat, atop the fleeing Poka and flattened him to the floor.

Grandfather Spirit turned triumphantly to Grandmother Spirit. "*That's* the fighting spirit! *That's* an emperor who can lead his troops into battle!"

Grandmother Spirit gave Grandfather Spirit a peck on the cheek. "If you say so."

Poka rose, disentangling himself from the angry ball of legs and fallen pants that held him captive. "See how this violent person assaulted me without cause?"

Grandfather Spirit adjusted Master Mapmaker's round spectacles on his nose. "Well, now. It does seem you are entitled to some justice."

"I should say so." Poka made a brave attempt to salvage his flattened hat.

"That person"—Grandmother Spirit pointed to Lumi, who was struggling to stand and losing the Battle of the Trousers—"seems to think the bird belongs to him."

"He's a violent lunatic," Poka said. "He belongs in the dungeons." He looked about the room. "If none of you can see reason, I appeal to the emperor himself."

"Oh, I wouldn't do that, if I were you." Begonia struggled to keep a straight face.

Poka turned toward Grandmother Spirit and Grandfather Spirit. "I beg you, venerable elders," he said. "My carnival isn't complete without its postrich. The people of Camellion need a carnival to bring them joy and laughter, and what's more comical than these huge birds? I ask you!"

He flapped out his arms, pretending they were ostrich

wings, stuck out his bottom, and waddled around, bobbing his head in a gifted impression of Lightfoot's ostrichy gait.

Everyone in the room laughed. Poka, ever the entertainer, forgot to be angry and hammed up his act even more.

Grandfather Spirit looked at Grandmother Spirit. "Should we?"

"We shouldn't." She winked at Begonia. "But I won't tell if you won't."

"Mr. Poka, sir," Grandfather Spirit called. "Have you any family?"

"None at all," said Poka.

"Except *your niece*, you mean," Begonia said wickedly.

"In that case, we agree with you," Grandfather Spirit called to Poka. "Your carnival desperately needs a 'postrich.'"

And with a snap of both ancestors' fingers, the proprietor of Poka's Carnival of Curiosities disappeared in a puff of red smoke. In his place stood a tall, handsome male ostrich, waddling and bobbing just as Poka had done.

Until Lightfoot saw him. A rival for Alfalfa's affections! He raised his wings in warning, hooted his battle cry, and charged the new "postrich" until it fled the room.

34

ONE MORE JOURNEY, AND PARTING GIFTS

"Mumsy?" said Begonia.

"Yes, my dear?"

"I have a favor to ask you."

"I'm listening."

They walked along the highway, each leading a cow by a rope. Chrysanthemumsy led a two-year-old milker, whom she'd decided to call Clover, and Begonia led Clover's calf, now named Corn. Corn wore the brass bell that the Seller of Many Things had given Begonia. It tinkled in the morning air. Stormcloud the cat had taken up a perch on Clover's neck and lounged there like a queen riding on her elephant.

"Well?" Mumsy prompted her.

"I'd like to be the one to name the sheep." Begonia bit her lip and waited for a reply.

"Oh?"

They turned to see Key, many paces behind, struggling to pull along the path two playful young ewes, one white and one black. Their lead ropes tangled as they capered.

Chrysanthemumsy turned back to Begonia. "What will you call them?"

Her daughter grinned. "Salt and Pepper."

"My goodness." Chrysanthemumsy smiled. "Spices instead of plants. That will take some getting used to."

Begonia bit into a juicy pear from the basket the kitchen chefs had packed them.

"Although . . ." Mumsy mused, "pepper *is* a plant . . ."

"I can't wait to tell Peony all that's happened," Begonia said. "She'll never believe it."

"You'll be quite the celebrity in her eyes now, having saved the empire." Mumsy winked at Begonia and pulled a sticky bun from the basket. "I'm glad Grandfather Spirit sent a message to let her know we were on our way home." She paused to swallow. "I expect she and Grandmother Flummox must have been terribly frightened when I didn't return."

"Were you frightened when I didn't come back that first night?" Begonia asked.

Mumsy pulled her close and kissed the crown of her daughter's head. Thank heavens she'd finally had a bath last night at the palace! Her hair was clean at last.

Their party had taken a merry leave of the palace that morning. The chancellor, Shoe the butler, and all the servants in the palace had gathered around to see them on their way, urging them to return soon. No one, however, wished for this more than Emperor Gowli the Seventh.

Tree, Song, and the baby accompanied them until they reached their cottage. Tree carried the baby the entire way. He sang loud, boisterous, and slightly naughty woodcutting songs, which made the baby laugh till tears streamed down his fat cheeks. Begonia, if she'd had to place a bet on it, couldn't have said who was happier, Song or Tree.

"I think Tree will make a fine father, don't you?" she said.

Mumsy smiled. "I wish them all the luck in the world. When we get home, let's make them a quilt as a wedding gift."

Begonia nodded. "We can take it to them when we take Key and Sprout back to Lotus City." She tossed her pear core to an expectant squirrel. "Oh! We'll take Peony, too, and show her the palace. She'll love that. I'll braid her hair up specially."

Mumsy smiled at that. "You know, Begonia," she said, "I think the emperor is going to miss you. You and Key just might be his first real friends."

"I'll miss him, too," Begonia said. "Though I have a feeling that in the future, the emperor will take a more active interest in the smaller towns and villages in Camellion. I'll bet he'll travel around more to see how things are going."

"Riding in on his ostrich, spreading truth and justice?" asked Mumsy.

Begonia grinned. "Something like that."

"Tell me more about your other new friend. Young Master Key."

They turned back to look at him. His arms formed an X across his body as Salt pulled toward the clover on one side of the road, and Pepper lunged for some daisies on the other side. He, too, had enjoyed a bath at the palace, and a feast of meatballs and noodle soup, and a night's sleep in a guest bedchamber. His bed pillows, however, hadn't survived the ordeal in top condition. Even now, Key's hair was so full of feathers he looked like a molting seagull.

"I think," Begonia said slowly, "that Key is like hot mustard. He takes a lot of getting used to."

Mumsy poked Begonia with her elbow. "I adore hot mustard."

"It has its uses." Begonia laughed. "Poor Poka."

Begonia turned back to watch Key nearly topple over from being tangled up with the sheep. "Key may never want to leave us," she warned her mother. "I think he envies me, just a little, for having the family I've got." She slipped her arm around her mother's waist. "I'm glad he's found Shoe. He has family that wants him now. But I'm not sure Key will ever look the part of a palace butler."

Mumsy nodded. "He does seem to have an owl growing out of his head. Well, he's welcome to stay as long as he likes. I owe that boy a great deal."

"The thing I think he wants most," Begonia said with a smile, "is home-cooked meals. Meatballs especially."

They came to the crossroads where Begonia had first met Song and her baby. She pointed out to her mother the purple flowering bush where she'd first met Key. Just then, Salt and Pepper gamboled forward and got their lead ropes tangled up in Clover's legs. Mumsy went back to help Key disentangle their animals, while Begonia wandered slowly on ahead.

Suddenly, she wasn't alone. A mustard cart that wasn't there before rattled beside her.

Begonia grinned. "Hello, Grandmother Spirit."

"Hello, dearie." Grandmother Spirit's mustard-maker face crinkled affectionately.

They walked along in silence for a while. Begonia waited for Grandmother Spirit to say something, but she didn't. Begonia wondered if she should supply the conversation, but what does one say to an ancient spirit, an honored ancestor, worshipped in temples throughout the empire? Ancestors, she considered, were nothing at all like she thought they were.

"Go ahead, dearie," said Grandmother Spirit. "Ask me the question you want answered."

Begonia looked up in surprise. "What question?"

Grandmother Spirit gazed deep into Begonia's eyes. *Oh. That question.* The one she'd lain up thinking about last night in her palace bedroom, long after Mumsy had fallen asleep.

Begonia stared at her feet. "It seems you know what it is," she said, "so there's not much point in my asking, is there?"

"Don't be a goose," scolded Grandmother Spirit. "Ask. It's what I'm here for. You can always, always ask. Remember that, my girl. Your whole life long, whoever you're with, whatever your question. Ask it."

"I'll try." Begonia tried to think. "Why did everyone see something different in Alfalfa's spot? Was it because you put a charm on her?"

Grandmother Spirit's eyes twinkled. "I had a bit of fun with that," she said, "but yes, it was the charm that did the trick." She tapped Begonia twice on the forehead. "But that, my girl, is not your question."

No, it wasn't her real question. But now, here, in the light of day, Begonia's real question seemed so petty, so foolish. She felt ashamed. "I don't even know how to start."

"Start smack in the middle," Grandmother Spirit advised, "and flounder around in circles for a while. That's what I do. Your meaning will tumble out eventually."

"All right." She took a deep breath. "It's just . . . back home, I always had to do everything. Well, almost everything. My sister, Peony, gets away with doing nothing. Practically nothing." She looked up to see if Grandmother Spirit was angry at her for this. It was true! Well, mostly true. "The reason I was the one who went after Alfalfa," she explained, "is the same reason I do everything else at home. Because I *can*. Because I *will*. Because I can be *counted on*."

Grandmother Spirit nodded. "Those are wonderful things, child."

Begonia frowned. "I'm not so sure. It seems to me that the reward for being a good girl is that you get asked to do everything for everyone else. And the people who do nothing are rewarded by having less expected of them. They get to make paper dolls with Mumsy while 'trustworthy Begonia' does everything." She glanced sidelong at Grandmother Spirit. "Well, mostly everything."

The mustard-maker's aged eyes watched her closely. "I'm still waiting for the question."

Begonia sighed.

"Is that why you chose me, too?" she said. "Did you send Alfalfa after the emperor's ostrich because *trustworthy Begonia* was the one who'd go? Will that person always have to be me?" Her eyes grew wet, and she rubbed them angrily on her sleeve. "Always the reliable one, getting kicked into the spilled milk, and shoveling out the cow poo, and getting lost, and being chased by panthers, while others get the things I want?" She sniffled miserably. "Paper dolls and hair ribbons and storytime by the fire?"

There. She'd said it all. There was nothing left except to be embarrassed and tired. "I don't really want paper dolls and hair ribbons. Not even. I just . . . you know what I mean."

She glanced back to see if there was any danger of Mumsy or Key overhearing her, but they were even farther back.

Reluctantly, she looked into Grandmother Spirit's eyes. Instead of judgment or criticism there, she saw only kindness.

"I do know what you mean," said Grandmother Spirit. "Some things are just unfair. There's no getting around it."

Begonia nodded and wiped her eyes again. Of course. She

knew that. The unfairness of life had made itself clear to her years and years ago.

"Know this, my girl: the things you're doing now, at this marvelous age in your life, aren't going to waste. All your reliable, responsible choices are building a brain, a heart, and a pair of hands ready to tackle anything life sends your way." Grandmother Spirit cradled Begonia's cheeks in her own soft, wrinkled hands. "The world will be so lucky to have your brain, heart, and hands in it."

Grandmother Spirit's face went blurry as tears swam in Begonia's eyes. Grandmother Spirit took the tail of the pink scarf she'd given her and gently dabbed the corners of her eyes with it.

"But also know this: the joyful things in life, the paper dolls and hair ribbons and absolutely the stories by the fire, are also choices that are open to you. You could choose them more often, my dear, and the important work would still get done."

Begonia wrapped her arms around Grandmother Spirit's neck without thinking. Only as she felt her warm embrace did she remember that this was a venerable ancestor. For all she knew, this might be an act of blasphemy. But if it was, Grandmother Spirit didn't seem to mind.

They walked farther down the road. "I think you'll find," Grandmother Spirit went on, "that Peony has been learning several new things about herself while you've been away.

First, how much she misses you. But second, she's learning how much more she can do than she knew she could." She smiled. "I should warn you. She's forming very strong opinions about chicken care. And she's already planted some of your seedlings."

"*What?*"

Grandmother Spirit shrugged. "What can you do? Some of her opinions, I should tell you, are quite sound. You should listen to her."

Begonia wrinkled her nose. Then she laughed. Behind them, she saw Mumsy and Key catching up to them.

"They can't see me right now, dearie," Grandmother Spirit said. "This little talk is just for us. But I need to go. Your mother has missed you so, and I shouldn't steal all your time with her."

"It's not stealing." Begonia winked. "It's borrowing."

Grandmother Spirit's face crinkled like a dried apple. "A girl in a million."

"Don't go," Begonia said. "Please."

Grandmother Spirit gave Begonia a peck on the cheek. "I'm never far. And that pot of mustard, you'll find, will last you a good long time. Good for your health. Good for all sorts of things. Even works as glue in a pinch."

Begonia saw her mother approaching, and ridiculous Key, and she smiled. She had her Mumsy back at last and had found a new friend to keep.

But Grandmother Spirit . . . would she ever see her again? She wished she could give her a gift in return.

She unraveled the pink scarf from around her neck. "Would you like this back?"

"Keep it," the ancestor spirit said as she faded out of sight, "to remember me by."

EPILOGUE:
AN OSTRICH MEETS
A POSTRICH

ORNING, IN THE PALACE PLEASURE gardens. One week later.

Lightfoot the ostrich sauntered around the lawn. Over on a shady knoll, Alfalfa mooed at him winsomely. She'd found a succulent patch of clover, but would come visit him presently. Meanwhile, a peacock strutted by, some distance away, fanning out his tail to a bored female, but the ostrich didn't mind him. Yards away, in the stream that burbled through the gardens, pairs of ducks and pelicans splashed and fished in the shallows. A stork flapped his way to a topmost tower, while an eagle screamed overhead, then swooped down to snatch a morsel of meat from the Keeper of the Imperial Aviary's gloved hand.

Lightfoot wasn't interested in these avian doings. He patrolled the grounds outside a long window. Inside, his man-chick stood looking over maps and papers with an old man with skinny limbs and a round belly. Rather like an ostrich, in fact. Lightfoot had decided to accept this older human. His man-chick seemed to like him, and he posed no apparent danger.

Across the lawns, near the gate in the high wall, a sound caught Lightfoot's ear. He stalked over to investigate. One never knew what might be a hidden threat to his man-chick. A jackal! A cobra! Ceaseless vigilance was the ostrich's only plan.

It was a tinkling sound. Lightfoot's head cocked to one side. Cobras didn't tinkle. At least, he was fairly sure they didn't.

The Keeper of the Imperial Aviary, too, had heard the noise and gone to the gate to investigate. He opened it, and a man stepped through, with a bit of rope clutched in one hand.

The man wore an earring that shone like a beetle's shell. His bald dome of a head reminded Lightfoot of an ostrich egg.

"Good morning," the man told the Keeper of the Imperial Aviary. "I'm a Seller of Many Things from the village of Two Windmills. A local farmer caught a bird and brought it to me. He figured I would know exactly whom to sell it to."

"Bird?" asked the keeper. "What kind of a bird?"

The egg-headed man gave his rope a tug. "Come on, then."

A male ostrich somewhat older than Lightfoot stepped

reluctantly through the gates and blinked in the sunlight. A little bell hung around his neck.

At the sight of the big bird, the keeper's eagle screeched. All the downy feathers on Lightfoot's neck stood on end. A threat! A rival! For his cow? For his man-chick? *We do not like this bad ostrich!*

But the keeper whistled. "What a beauty!"

"Do you think the emperor will want him?" asked the Seller of Many Things.

"I know he will," answered the birdman. "He's uncommonly fond of ostriches. And he plans to open up the aviary, and all the menagerie, to the public, so I know he'll be glad to have another big bird to show the children." He reached into his pocket and pulled out some coins. "I'll give you fifteen silver buckles for him."

The egg-man nodded. "Sold. He's all yours."

"I can't imagine how a loose ostrich could be roaming the countryside of Camellion, though," said the Keeper of the Imperial Aviary. "Nobody else keeps them but the emperor."

"I thought of selling him to that traveling carnival," said the salesman, "but they seem to have scattered and closed up shop. Did you ever lose an ostrich?"

"Only briefly. He's back now. Aren't you, Lightfoot? Come on, meet your new friend. Don't be shy."

But Lightfoot wasn't so easily fooled. He ballooned out his neck and hooted a low honk of warning to the bad ostrich.

"Don't be testy, Lightfoot," scolded the keeper. "Come along, new fellow. Wait till my master sees you!"

The man with the shiny egg for a head took his leave. The keeper led the new bird onto the grounds and shut the gate. Then he took the new ostrich to the aviary, followed at every step by a suspicious Lightfoot, and offered him food and water. The new ostrich had an odd gait to his walk, as though he wasn't used to having such long legs. His head bobbed side to side as if his neck was something he was still getting used to. All the more reason, Lightfoot felt, not to trust him. Something about him just wasn't right.

The new bird was more interested in the palace than in breakfast. He left the aviary and waddled over to the palace window where Lightfoot's man-chick studied papers on a table and stroked an orange kitten. The curious bird pecked the window with his beak.

That was enough for Lightfoot. He spread his wings and charged the bad bird. The bad bird fled back to the safety of the aviary and stood quivering behind its keeper.

"Come now, Lightfoot, make friends," the keeper said soothingly. "There's plenty of room here. Show him around, introduce him to the peacocks. Don't be jealous. There's no reason you can't both be the emperor's ostrich."

ACKNOWLEDGMENTS

WHEN I SET OUT TO WRITE FOR YOUNG readers, dreaming of holding a book with my name on the spine, I had no idea that the real payoff would be the chance to teach schoolchildren what reading and writing mean to me. It's been my delight to help students see that anyone can conjure up an idea, fling it down on paper, and roll around in it for a while, grammar rules be hanged! Seeing students who feel thwarted by writing's technicalities discover the power that comes when *nobody can tell you that your imagination is wrong* is reason enough to keep on tapping at my own keyboard.

Margaret Lazenby, Karen Duff, and Sara Apke were the first to invite me to present to students, and I'll be forever grateful. Sara asked me to develop not just an assembly but a classroom workshop. It was during a workshop at her school that the idea for this book was born.

Larissa Theule and Catherine Linka, my weekly writing buddies, kept me sane and on track during the chaotic season of this book's incubation. It was Catherine, inviting me to give an audacious presentation on how writers can get themselves "Unstuck," who handed me the tools I needed to steer this manuscript through its forest of panthers. My agent, Alyssa Henkin, deserves a Good Humor medal for supporting every wacky idea I toss her way, and my editor, Katherine Jacobs, cheerfully came along on this ostrich chase. Special thanks also to Noa Wheeler and to Elizabeth H. Clark.

Carrie Salisbury and Ginger Johnson made sure I was fed, body and spirit. My discerning early readers, Deborah Kovacs, Ammi-Joan Paquette, Nancy Werlin, and my dashing son Daniel, laughed in all the right places. My Phil did the same. Like Song, I knew from day one that he was the woodcutter for me and would be a splendid holder of babies. No love charm required.